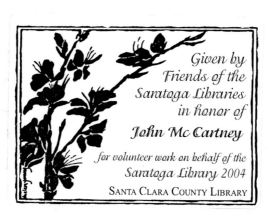

Given by
Friends of the
Saratoga Libraries
in honor of

John Mc Cartney

for volunteer work on behalf of the
Saratoga Library 2004

SANTA CLARA COUNTY LIBRARY

Also by Joy Williams

FICTION

State of Grace
Taking Care: Stories
The Changeling
Breaking and Entering
Escapes: Stories
The Quick and the Dead

NONFICTION

The Florida Keys: A History and Guide
Ill Nature: Essays

HONORED GUEST

Williams, Joy, 1944–
Honored guest : stories
/
2004.
33305207577812
sa   12/08/04

HONORED GUEST

—Stories—

JOY WILLIAMS

ALFRED A. KNOPF   NEW YORK   2004

SANTA CLARA COUNTY LIBRARY

3 3305 20757 7812

THIS IS A BORZOI BOOK
PUBLISHED BY ALFRED A. KNOPF

Copyright © 2004 by Joy Williams
All rights reserved under International and Pan-American Copyright
Conventions. Published in the United States by Alfred A. Knopf,
a division of Random House, Inc., New York, and simultaneously
in Canada by Random House of Canada Limited, Toronto.
Distributed by Random House, Inc., New York.

www.aaknopf.com
Knopf, Borzoi Books, and the colophon are registered trademarks of
Random House, Inc.

"Charity" appeared originally in the *Atlantic Monthly;* "The Visiting Privilege"
and "Hammer" in *Conjunctions;* "Honored Guest" in *Harper's;* "Marabou"
and "Substance" in *The Paris Review;* "Anodyne" in *Story;* and "Fortune"
in *Tin House.* "Congress" originally appeared in the anthology *Leopard II,*
edited by Christopher Maclehose (London: Harvill Press, 1993).

Library of Congress Cataloging-in-Publication Data
Williams, Joy, [date]
Honored guest : stories / Joy Williams — 1st ed.
p.   cm.
Contents: Honored guest—Congress—Marabou—The visiting
privilege—Substance—Anodyne—The other week—Claro—
Charity—ACK—Hammer—Fortune.
ISBN 0-679-44647-8 (alk. paper)
1. Parent and adult child—Fiction. 2. Conflict of generations—Fiction.
3. Domestic fiction, American. I. Title.
PS3573.I4496H66 2004
813'.54—dc22
2004044199

Manufactured in the United States of America
First Edition

CONTENTS

· · ·

HONORED GUEST

HONORED GUEST

SHE HAD BEEN HAVING a rough time of it and thought about suicide sometimes, but suicide was so corny and you had to be careful in this milieu which was eleventh grade because two of her classmates had committed suicide the year before and between them they left twenty-four suicide notes and had become just a joke. They had left the notes everywhere and they were full of misspellings and pretensions. Theirs had been a false show. Then this year a girl had taken an overdose of Tylenol which of course did nothing at all, but word of it got out and when she came back to school her locker had been broken into and was full of Tylenol, just jammed with it. Like, you moron. Under the circumstances, it was amazing that Helen thought of suicide at all. It was just not cool. You only made a fool of yourself. And the parents of these people were mocked too. They were considered to be suicide-enhancing, evil and weak, and they were ignored and barely tolerated. This was a small town. Helen didn't want to make it any harder on her mother than circumstances already had.

Her mother was dying and she wanted to die at home, which Helen could understand, she understood it perfectly, she'd say, but actually she understood it less well than that and it had become clear it wasn't even what needed to be understood. Nothing needed to be understood.

There was a little brass bell on her mother's bedside table. It was the same little brass bell that had been placed at Helen's command when she had been a little girl, sick with some harmless little kid's sickness. She had just to reach out her hand and ring the bell and her mother would come or even her father. Her mother never used the bell now and kept it there as sort of a joke, actually. Her mother was not utterly confined to bed. She moved around a bit at night and placed herself, or was placed by others, in other rooms during the day. Occasionally one of the women who had been hired to care for her during the day would even take her for a drive, out to see the icicles or go to the bank window. Her mother's name was Lenore and sometimes in the night her mother would call out this name, her own, "Lenore!" in a strong, urgent voice and Helen in her own room would shudder and cry a little.

This had been going on for a while. In the summer Lenore had been diagnosed and condemned but she kept bouncing back, as the doctors put it, until recently. The daisies that bloomed in the fall down by the storm-split elm had come and gone, even the little kids at Halloween. Thanksgiving had passed without comment and it would be Christmas soon. Lenore was ignoring it. The boxes of balls and lights were in the cellar, buried deep. Helen had made the horrible mistake of asking her what she wanted for Christmas one night and Lenore had said, "Are you stupid?" Then she said, "Oh, I don't mean to be so impatient, it's the medicine, my voice doesn't even sound right. Does my voice sound right? Get me something you'll want later. A piece of jewelry or something. Do you want the money for it?" She meant this sincerely.

At the beginning they had talked eagerly like equals. This was more important than a wedding, this preparation. They even laughed like girls together remembering things. They remembered when Helen was a little girl before the divorce and they were all driving somewhere and Helen's father was stopped for speeding and Lenore wanted her picture taken with the policeman and Helen had taken it. "Wasn't that mean!" Lenore said to Helen.

When Lenore died, Helen would go down to Florida and live with her father. "I've never had the slightest desire to visit Florida," Lenore would say. "You can have it."

At the beginning, death was giving them the opportunity to be interesting. This was something special. There was only one crack at this. But then they lost sight of it somehow. It became a lesser thing, more terrible. Its meaning crumbled. They began waiting for it. Terrible, terrible. Lenore had friends but they called now, they didn't come over so much. "Don't come over," Lenore would tell them, "it wears me out." Little things started to go wrong with the house, leaks and lights. The bulb in the kitchen would flutter when the water was turned on. Helen grew fat for some reason. The dog, their dog, began to change. He grew shy. "Do you think he's acting funny?" Lenore asked Helen.

She did not tell Helen that the dog had begun to growl at her. It was a secret growl, he never did it in front of anyone else.

He had taken to carrying one of her slippers around with him. He was almost never without it. He cherished her slipper.

"Do you remember when I put Grecian Formula on his muzzle because he turned gray so young?" Lenore said. "He was only about a year old and began to turn gray? The things I used to do. The way I spent my time."

But now she did not know what to do with time at all. It seemed more expectant than ever. One couldn't satisfy it, one could never do enough for it.

She was so uneasy.

Lenore had a dream in which she wasn't dying at all. Someone else had died. People had told her this over and over again. And now they were getting tired of reminding her, impatient.

She had a dream of eating bread and dying. Two large loaves. Pounds of it, still warm from the oven. She ate it all, she was so hungry, starving! But then she died. It was the bread. It was too hot, was the explanation. There were people in her room but she was not among them.

When she woke, she could feel the hot, gummy, almost liquid bread in her throat, scalding it. She lay in bed on her side, her dark eyes open. It was four o'clock in the morning. She swung her legs to the floor. The dog growled at her. He slept in her room with her slipper but he growled as she made her way past him. Sometimes self-pity would rise within her and she would stare at the dog, tears in her eyes, listening to him growl. The more she stared, the more sustained was his soft growl.

She had a dream about a tattoo. This was a pleasant dream. She was walking away and she had the most beautiful tattoo covering her shoulders and back, even the back of her legs. It was unspeakably fine.

Helen had a dream that her mother wanted a tattoo. She wanted to be tattooed all over, a full custom bodysuit, but no one would do it. Helen woke protesting this, grunting and cold. She had kicked off her blankets. She pulled them up and curled tightly beneath them. There was a boy at school who had gotten a tattoo and now they wouldn't let him play basketball.

In the morning Lenore said, "Would you get a tattoo with me? We could do this together. I don't think it's creepy," she added. "I think you'll be glad later. A pretty one, just small somewhere. What do you think?" The more she considered it, the more it seemed the perfect thing to do. What else could be done? She'd already given Helen her wedding ring.

"I'll get him to come over here, to the house. I'll arrange it," Lenore said. Helen couldn't defend herself against this notion. She still felt sleepy, she was always sleepy. There was something wrong with her mother's idea but not much.

But Lenore could not arrange it. When Helen returned from school, her mother said, "It can't be done. I'm so upset and I've lost interest so I'll give you the short version. I called . . . I must have made twenty calls. At last I got someone to speak to me. His name was Smokin' Joe and he was a hundred miles away but sounded as though he'd do it. And I asked him if there was any place he didn't tattoo, and he said faces, dicks and hands."

"Mom!" Helen said. Her face reddened.

"And I asked him if there was any*one* he wouldn't tattoo, and he said drunks and the dying. So that was that."

"But you didn't have to tell him. You won't have to tell him," Helen said.

"That's true," Lenore said dispiritedly. Then she looked angrily at Helen. "Are you crazy? Sometimes I think you're crazy!"

"Mom!" Helen said, crying. "I want you to do what you want."

"This was my idea, mine!" Lenore said. The dog gave a high nervous bark. "Oh dear," Lenore said, "I'm speaking too loudly." She smiled at him as if to say how clever both of them were to realize this.

That night Lenore could not sleep. There were no dreams, nothing. High clouds swept slowly past the window. She got up and went into the living room, to the desk there. She looked with distaste at all the objects in this room. There wasn't one thing here she'd want to take with her to the grave, not one. The dog had shuffled out of the bedroom with her and now lay at her feet, a slipper in his mouth, a red one with a little bow. She wanted to make note of a few things, clarify some things. She took out a piece of paper. The furnace turned on and she heard something moving behind the walls. "Enjoy it while you can," she said. She sat at the desk, her back very straight, waiting for something. After a while she looked at the dog. "Give me that," she said. "Give me that slipper." He growled but did not leave her side. She took a pen and wrote on the paper, *When I go, the dog goes. Promise me this.* She left it out for Helen.

Then she thought, That dog is the dumbest one I've ever had. I don't want him with me. She was amazed she could still think like this. She tore up the piece of paper. "Lenore!" she cried, and wrung her hands. She wanted herself. Her mind ran stumbling, panting, through dark twisted woods.

When Helen got up she would ask her to make some toast.

Toast would taste good. Helen would press the *Good Morning* letters on the bread. It was a gadget, like a cookie cutter. When the bread was toasted, the words were pressed down into it and you dribbled honey into them.

In the morning Helen did this carefully, as she always had. They sat together at the kitchen table and ate the toast. Sleet struck the windows. Helen looked at her toast dreamily, the golden letters against the almost black. They both liked their toast almost black.

Lenore felt peaceful. She even felt a little better. But it was a cruelty to feel a little better, a cruelty to Helen.

"Turn on the radio," Lenore said, "and find out if they're going to cancel school." If Helen stayed home today she would talk to her. Important things would be said. Things that would still matter years and years from now.

Callers on a talk show were speaking about wolves. "There should be wolf control," someone said, "not wolf worship."

"Oh, I hate these people," Helen said.

"Are you a wolf worshipper?" her mother asked. "Watch out."

"I believe they have the right to live too," Helen said fervently. Then she was sorry. Everything she said was wrong. She moved the dial on the radio. School would not be canceled. They never canceled it.

"There's a stain on that blouse," her mother said. "Why do your clothes always look so dingy? You should buy some new clothes."

"I don't want any new clothes," Helen said.

"You can't wear mine, that's not the way to think. I've got to get rid of them. Maybe that's what I'll do today. I'll go through them with Jean. It's Jean who comes today, isn't it?"

9

"I don't want your clothes!"

"Why not? Not even the sweaters?"

Helen's mouth trembled.

"Oh, what are we going to do!" Lenore said. She clawed at her cheeks. The dog barked.

"Mom, Mom," Helen said.

"We've got to talk, I want to talk," Lenore said. What would happen to Helen, her little girl . . .

Helen saw the stain her mother had noticed on the blouse. Where had it come from? It had just appeared. She would change if she had time.

"When I die, I'm going to forget you," Lenore began. This was so obvious, this wasn't what she meant. "The dead just forget you. The most important things, all the loving things, everything we . . ." She closed her eyes, then opened them with effort. "I want to put on some lipstick today," she said. "If I don't, tell me when you come home."

Helen left just in time to catch the bus. Some of her classmates stood by the curb, hooded, hunched. It was bitter out.

In the house, Lenore looked at the dog. There were only so many dogs in a person's life and this was the last one in hers. She'd like to kick him. But he had changed when she'd gotten sick, he hadn't been like this before. He was bewildered. He didn't like it—death—either. She felt sorry for him. She went back into her bedroom and he followed her with the slipper.

At nine, the first in a number of nurse's aides and companions arrived. By three it was growing dark again. Helen returned before four.

"The dog needs a walk," her mother said.

"It's so icy out, Mom, he'll cut the pads of his feet."

"He needs to go out!" her mother screamed. She wore a little lipstick and sat in a chair wringing her hands.

Helen found the leash and coaxed the dog to the door. He looked out uneasily into the wet cold blackness. They moved out into it a few yards to a bush he had killed long before and he dribbled a few drops of urine onto it. They walked a little farther, across the dully shining yard toward the street. It was still, windless. The air made a hissing sound. "Come on," Helen said, "don't you want to do something?" The dog walked stoically along. Helen's eyes began to water with the cold. Her mother had said, "I want Verdi played at the service, Scriabin, no hymns." Helen had sent away for some recordings. How else could it be accomplished, the Verdi, the Scriabin . . . Once she had called her father and said, "What should we do for Mom?"

"Where have you been!" her mother said when they got back. "My God, I thought you'd been hit by a truck."

They ate supper, macaroni and cheese, something one of the women had prepared. Lenore ate without speaking and then looked at the empty plate.

"Do you want some more, Mom?" Helen asked.

"One of those girls that comes, she says she'll take the dog," Lenore said.

Helen swallowed. "I think it would be good," she said.

"That's it then. She'll take him tomorrow."

"Is she just going to see how it works out or what?"

"No, she wants him. She lives in an iffy neighborhood and the dog, you know, can be impressive when he wants. I think better now than later. He's only five, five next month." She knew the dog's birthday. She laughed at this.

The next day, when Helen came home from school the dog was gone. His bowls were gone from the corner near the sink.

"At least I have my slipper back," Lenore said. She had it in her hand, the red slipper.

Helen was doing her homework. She was a funny kid, Lenore thought, there she was doing her homework.

"It's almost over for me," Lenore said. "I'm at the end of my life."

Helen looked up. "Mom," she said.

"I can't believe it."

"I'm a nihilist," Helen said. "That's what I'm going to be."

"You can't think you're going to be a nihilist," her mother said. "Are you laughing at me? Don't you dare laugh at me. I'm still your mother." She shook her fist.

"Mom, Mom," Helen said, "I'm not laughing." She began to cry.

"Don't cry," Lenore said dully.

Helen looked down at her textbook. She had underlined everything on one page. Everything! Stupid . . . She'd be stupid in Florida too, she thought. She could think about Florida only by being here with her mother. Otherwise Florida didn't really exist.

Lenore said, "God is nothing. OK? That's Meister Eckehart. But whatever is not God is nothing and ought to be accounted as nothing. OK? That's someone else."

Helen didn't speak.

"I wasn't born yesterday," her mother said. "That's why I know these things. I wasn't even born last night." She laughed. It was snowing again. It had been snowing freshly for hours. First sleet, then colder, then this snow.

"Helen," her mother said, "would you get me a snowball? Go out and make me one and bring it back."

Helen got up and went outside as though hypnotized. Sometimes she behaved like this, as though she were an unwilling yet efficient instrument. She could have thoughts and not think them. She was protected, at the same time she was helping her mother do her job, the job being this peculiar business.

The snow was damp and lovely. Huge flakes softly struck her face and felt like living things. She went past the bush the dog had liked, pushed her hands deeply into the snow and made a snowball for her mother, perfect as an orange.

Lenore studied this. "This is good snow, isn't it?" she said. "Perfect snow." She packed it tighter and threw it across the room at Helen. It hit her squarely in the chest.

"Oh!" Lenore exclaimed.

"That hurt, Mom," Helen said.

"Oh you . . ." Lenore said. "Get me another."

"No!" Helen said. The thing had felt like a rock. Her breasts hurt. Her mother was grinning avidly at her.

"Get two, come on," her mother said. "We'll have a snowball fight in the house. Why not!"

"No!" Helen said. "This is . . . you're just pretending . . ."

Lenore looked at her. She pulled her bathrobe tighter around herself. "I'm going to go to bed," she said.

"Do you want me to make some tea?" Helen said. "Let me make some tea."

"Tea, tea," Lenore mimicked. "What will you drink in Florida? You'll drink iced tea."

That night Lenore dreamed she was on a boat with others. A white boat in clear, lovely water. They were moving quickly

13

but there was a banging sound, arrhythmic, incessant, sad, it was sad. It's the banger, they said, the fish too big for the box, that's what we call them. Let it go, Lenore begged. Too late now, they said, too late for it now.

"Lenore!" she cried. She went into Helen's room. Helen slept with the light on, her radio playing softly, books scattered on her bed.

"Sleep with me," her mother said.

Helen shrank back. "I can't, please," she said.

"My God, you won't lie down with me!" her mother said. She had things from Helen's childhood still—little nightgowns, coloring books, valentines.

"All right, all right," Helen said. Her eyes were wild, she looked blinded.

"No, all right, forget it," Lenore said. She shook her head from side to side, panting. Helen's room was almost bare. There were no pictures, no pretty things, not even a mirror. Plastic was stapled to the window frames to keep out the cold. When had this happened? Lenore wondered. Tomorrow, she thought. She shouldn't try to say anything at night. Words at night were feral things. She limped back to her room. Her feet were swollen, discolored, water oozed from them. She would hide them. But where would she hide them? She sat up in bed, the pillows heaped behind her back, and watched them. They became remote, indecipherable.

It became morning again. *Mother . . . Earth . . .* said someone on the radio.

"An egg?" Helen asked. "Do you want an egg this morning?"

"You should get your hair cut today," Lenore said. "Go to the beauty parlor."

"Oh, Mom, it's all right."

"Get it trimmed or something. It needs something."

"But nobody will be here with you," Helen said. "You'll be home by yourself."

"Go after school. I can take care of myself for an hour. Something wouldn't happen in an hour, do you think?" Lenore felt sly saying this. Then she said, "I want you to look pretty, to feel good about yourself."

"I really hate those places," Helen said.

"Can't you do anything for me!" Lenore said.

Helen got off the bus at a shopping mall on the way back from school. "I don't have a reservation," she told the woman at the desk.

"You mean an appointment," the woman said. "You don't have an appointment."

She was taken immediately to a chair in front of a long mirror. The women in the chairs beside her were all looking into the mirror while their hairdressers stared into it too and cut their hair. Everyone was chatting and relaxed, but Helen didn't know how to do this, even this, this simple thing.

Sometimes Helen dreamed that she was her own daughter. She was free, self-absorbed, unfamiliar. Helen took up very little of her thoughts. But she could not pretend this.

She looked at the woman beside her, who had long wet hair and was smoking a cigarette. Above her shoe was a black parole anklet.

"These things don't work at all," the woman said. "I could take the damn thing off but I think it's kind of stylish. Often I do take the damn thing off and it's in one place and I'm in another. *Quite* another."

"What did you do?" Helen asked.

"I didn't do anything!" the woman bawled. Then she laughed. She dropped her cigarette in the cup of coffee she was holding.

The washing, the cutting, the drying, all this took a long time. Her hairdresser was an Asian named Mickey. "How old do you think I am?" Mickey asked.

"Twenty," Helen said. She did not look at her, or herself, in the mirror. She kept her eyes slightly unfocused, the way a dog would.

"I am thirty-five," Mickey said delightedly. "I am one-eighteenth Ainu. Do you know anything about the Ainu?"

Helen knew it wasn't necessary to reply to this. Someone several chairs away said in disbelief, "She's naming the baby *what?*"

"The Ainu are an aboriginal people of north Japan. Up until a little while ago they used to kill a bear in a sacred ritual each year. The anthropologists were wild about this ritual and were disappointed when they quit, but here goes, I will share it with you. At the end of each winter they'd catch a bear cub and give it to a woman to nurse. Wow, that's something! After it was weaned, it was given wonderful food and petted and played with. It was caged, but in all other respects it was treated as an honored guest. But the day always came when the leader of the village would come and tell the bear sorrowfully that it must be killed though they loved it dearly. This was this long oration, this part. Then everyone dragged the bear from its cage with ropes, tied it to a stake, shot it with blunt arrows that merely tortured it, then scissored its neck between two poles where it slowly strangled, after which they skinned it, decapitated it and offered the severed head some of its own flesh.

What do you think, do you think they knew what they were doing?"

"Was there something more to it than that?" Helen said. "Did something come after that?" She really was a serious girl. Her head burned from the hair dryer Mickey was wielding dramatically.

"These are my people!" Mickey said, ignoring her. "You've come a long way, baby! Maine or Bust!" She sounded bitter. She turned off the dryer, removed Helen's smock and with a little brush whisked her shoulders. "Ask for Mickey another time," she said. "That's me. Happy Holidays."

Helen paid and walked out into the cold. The cold felt delicious on her head. "An honored guest," she said aloud. To live was like being an honored guest. The thought was outside her, large and calm. Then you were no longer an honored guest. The thought turned away from her and faded.

Her mother was watching television with the sound off when Helen got home. "That's a nice haircut," her mother said. "Now don't touch it, don't pull at it like that for godssakes. It's pretty. You're pretty."

It was a ghastly haircut, really. Helen's large ears seemed to float, no longer quite attached to her head. Lenore gazed quietly at her.

"Mom," Helen said, "do you know there's a patron saint of television?"

Lenore thought this was hysterical.

"It's true," Helen said. "St. Clare."

Lenore wondered how long it would take for Helen's hair to grow back.

Later they were eating ice cream. They were both in their

nightgowns. Helen was reading a Russian novel. She loved Russian novels. Everyone was so emotional, so tormented. They clutched their heads, they fainted, they swooned, they galloped around. The snow. Russian snow had made Maine snow puny to Helen, meaningless.

"This ice cream tastes bad," her mother said. "It tastes like bleach or something." Some foul odor crept up her throat. Helen continued to read. Anyway, what were they doing eating ice cream in the middle of winter? Lenore wondered. It was laziness. Something was creeping quietly all through her. She'd like to jump out of her skin, she would.

"You now," she said, "I believe that if Jesus walked into this house this minute, you wouldn't even raise your eyes."

Helen bit her lip and reluctantly put down the book. "Oh, Mom," she said.

"And maybe you'd be right. I bet he'd lack charisma. I'd bet my last dollar on it. The only reason he was charismatic before was that those people lived in a prerational time."

"Jesus isn't going to walk in here, Mom, come on," Helen said.

"Well, something is, something big. You'd better be ready for it." She was angry. "You've got the harder road," she said finally. "You've got to behave in a way you won't be afraid to remember, but you know what my road is? My road is the *new* road."

Like everyone, Lenore had a dread of being alone in the world, forgotten by God, overlooked. There were billions upon billions of people, after all, it wasn't out of the question.

"The new road?" Helen asked.

"Oh, there's nothing new about it," Lenore said, annoyed. She stroked her own face with her hands. She shouldn't be doing this to Helen, her little Helen. But Helen was so docile. She wasn't fighting this! You had to fight.

"Go back to what you were doing," Lenore said. "You were reading, you were concentrating. I wish I could concentrate. My mind just goes from one thing to another. Do you know what I was thinking of, did I ever tell you this? When I was still well, before I went to the doctor? I was in a department store looking at a coat and I must have stepped in front of this woman who was looking at coats too. I had no idea . . . and she just started to stare at me. I was very aware of it but I ignored it for a long time, I even moved away. But she followed me, still staring. Until I finally looked at her. She still stared but now she was looking through me, *through* me, and she began talking to someone, resuming some conversation with whoever was with her, and all the while she was staring at me to show how insignificant I was, how utterly insignificant . . ." Lenore leaned toward Helen but then drew back, dizzy. "And I felt cursed. I felt as though she'd cursed me."

"What a weirdo," Helen said.

"I wonder where she picked that up," Lenore said. "I'd like to see her again. I'd like to murder her."

"I would too," Helen said. "I really would."

"No, murder's too good for that one," Lenore said. "Murder's for the elect. I think of murder . . . sometimes I think I wish someone would murder me. Out of the blue, without warning, for no reason. I wouldn't believe it was happening. It would be like not dying at all."

Helen sat in her nightgown. She felt cold. People had written books about death. No one knew what they were talking about, of course.

"Oh, I'm tired of talk," Lenore said. "I don't want to talk

anymore. I'm tired of thinking about it. Why do we have to think about it all the time! One of those philosophers said that Death was the Big Thinker. It thinks the instant that was your life, right down to the bottom of it."

"Which one?" Helen asked.

"Which one what?"

"Which philosopher?"

"I can't recall," Lenore said. Sometimes Helen amused her, she really amused her.

Lenore didn't dream that night. She lay in bed panting. She wasn't ready but there was nothing left to be done. The day before the girl had washed and dried the bedsheets and before she put them on again she had ironed them. Ironed them! They were just delicious, still delicious. It was the girl who loved to iron. She'd iron anything. What's-her-name. Lenore got up and moved through the rooms of the house uncertainly. She could hardly keep her balance. Then she went down into the cellar. Her heart was pounding, it felt wet and small in her chest. She looked at the oil gauge on the furnace. It was a little over one-quarter full. She wasn't going to order any more, she'd just see what happened. She barely had the strength to get back upstairs. She turned on the little lamp that was on the breakfast table and sat in her chair there, waiting for Helen. She saw dog hairs on the floor, gathering together, drifting across the floor.

Helen felt sick but she would drag herself to school. Her throat was sore. She heated up honey in a pan and sipped it with a spoon.

"I'm going to just stay put today," Lenore said.

"That's good, Mom, just take it easy. You've been doing too

much." Helen's forehead shone with sweat. She buttoned up her sweater with trembling fingers.

"Do you have a cold?" her mother said. "Where did you get a cold? Stay home. The nurse who's coming this afternoon, she can take a look at you and write a prescription. Look at you, you're sweating. You've probably got a fever." She wanted to weep for her little Helen.

"I have a test today, Mom," Helen said.

"A test," Lenore marveled. She laughed. "Take them now but don't take them later, they don't do you any good later."

Helen wiped at her face with a dish towel.

"My god, a dish towel!" Lenore said. "What's wrong with you? My god, what's to become of you!"

Startled, Helen dropped the towel. She expected to see her face on it almost. That was what had alarmed her mother so, that Helen had wiped off her own face. Anyone knew better than to do that . . . She felt faint. She was thinking of the test, of taking it in a few hours. She took a fresh dish towel from a drawer and put it on the rack.

"What if I die today?" Lenore said suddenly. "I want you to be with me. My god, I don't want to be alone."

"All this week there are tests," Helen said.

"Why don't I wait then?" Lenore said.

Tears ran down Helen's cheeks. She stood there stubbornly, looking at her mother.

"You were always able to turn them on and off," Lenore said, "just like a faucet. Crocodile tears." But with a moan she clutched her. Then she pulled away. "We have to wash these things," she said. "We can't just leave them in the sink." She seized the smudged glass she'd used to swallow her pills and rinsed it in running water. She held it up to the window and it slipped from her fingers and smashed against the sill. It was dirty and whole, she thought, and now it is clean and broken. This seemed to her, profound.

"Don't touch it!" she screamed. "Leave it for Barbara. Is that her name, Barbara?" Strangers, they were all strangers. "She never knows what to do when she comes."

"I have to go, Mom," Helen said.

"You do, of course you do," her mother said. She patted Helen's cheeks clumsily. "You're so hot, you're sick."

"I love you," Helen said.

"I love you too," Lenore said. Then she watched her walk down the street toward the corner. The day was growing lighter. The mornings kept coming, she didn't like it.

On the bus, the driver said to Helen, "I lost my mother when I was your age. You've just got to hang in there."

Helen walked toward the rear of the bus and sat down. She shut her eyes. A girl behind her snapped her gum and said, "'Hang in there.' What an idiot."

The bus pounded down the snow-packed streets.

The girl with the gum had been the one who told Helen how ashes came back. Her uncle had died and his ashes had come in a red shellacked box. It looked cheap but it had cost fifty-five dollars and there was an envelope taped to the box with his name typed on it beneath a glassine window as though he was being addressed to himself. This girl considered herself to be somewhat of an authority on the way these things were handled, for she had also lost a couple of godparents and knew how things were done as far south as Boston.

CONGRESS

MIRIAM WAS LIVING with a man named Jack Dewayne who taught a course in forensic anthropology at the state's university. It was the only program in the country that offered a certificate in forensic anthropology, as far as anyone knew, and his students adored him. They called themselves Deweenies and wore skull-and-crossbones T-shirts to class. People were mad for Jack in this town. Once, in a grocery store, when Miriam stood gazing into a bin of little limes, a woman came up to her and said, "Your Jack is a wonderful, wonderful man."

"Oh, thanks," Miriam said.

"My son Ricky disappeared four years ago and some skeletal remains were found at the beginning of this year. Scattered, broken, lots of bones missing, not much to go on, a real jumble. The officials told me they probably weren't Ricky's but your Jack told me they were, and with compassion he showed me how he reached that conclusion." The woman waited. In her cart was a big bag of birdseed and a bottle of vodka. "If it weren't for Jack, my Ricky's body would probably be unnamed still," she said.

"Well, thank you very much," Miriam said.

She never knew what to say to Jack's fans. As for them, they didn't understand Miriam at all. Why her of all people? With his hunger for life, Jack could have chosen better, they felt. Miriam lacked charm, they felt. She was gloomy. Even Jack found her gloomy occasionally.

Mornings, out in the garden, she would, at times, read aloud from one of her many overdue library books. Dew as radiant as angel spit glittered on the petals of Jack's roses. Jack was quite the gardener. Miriam thought she knew why he particularly favored roses. The inside of a rose does not at all correspond to its exterior beauty. If one tears off all the petals of the corolla, all that remains is a sordid-looking tuft. Roses would be right up Jack's alley, all right.

"Here's something for you, Jack," Miriam said. "You'll appreciate this. Beckett described tears as 'liquefied brain.'"

"God, Miriam," Jack said. "Why are you sharing that with me? Look at this day, it's a beautiful day! Stop pumping out the cesspit! Leave the cesspit alone!"

Then the phone would ring and Jack would begin his daily business of reconstructing the previous lives of hair and teeth when they had been possessed by someone. A detective a thousand miles away would send him a box of pitted bones and within days Jack would be saying, "This is a white male between the ages of twenty-five and thirty who didn't do drugs and who was tall, healthy and trusting. Too trusting, clearly."

Or a hand would be found in the stomach of a shark hauled up by a party boat off the Gulf coast of Florida and Jack would be flown off to examine it. He would return deeply tanned and refreshed, with a crisp new haircut, saying, "The shark was most certainly attracted to the rings on this hand. This is a teen's hand. She was small, perhaps even a legal midget, and well nourished. She was a loner, adventurous, not well educated and probably unemployed. Odds are the rings were stolen. She would certainly have done herself a favor by passing up the temptation of those rings."

Miriam hated it when Jack was judgmental and Jack was judgmental a great deal. She herself stole on occasion, mostly sheets. For some reason, it was easy to steal sheets. As a girl she had wanted to become a witty, lively and irresistible woman, skilled in repartee and in arguments on controversial subjects, but it hadn't turned out that way. She had become a woman who was still waiting for her calling.

Jack had no idea that Miriam stole sheets and more. He liked Miriam. He liked her bones. She had fine bones and he loved tracing them at night beneath her warm, smooth skin, her jawbone, collarbone, pelvic bone. It wasn't anything that consumed him, but he just liked her was all, usually. And he liked his work. He liked wrapping things up and dealing with those whom the missing had left behind. He was neither doctor nor priest; he was the forensic anthropologist, and he alone could give these people peace. They wanted to know, they had to know. Was that tibia in the swamp Denny's? Denny, we long to claim you . . . Were those little bits and pieces they got when they dragged the lake Lucile's even though she was supposed to be in Manhattan? She had told us she was going to be in Manhattan, there was never any talk about a lake . . . Bill had gone on a day hike years ago with his little white dog and now something had been found, found in a ravine at last . . . Pookie had toddled away from the Airstream on the Fourth of

July just as we were setting up the grill, she would be so much older now, a little girl instead of a baby, and it would be so good just to know, if we could only know . . .

And Jack would give them his gift. He could give them the incontrovertible and almost unspeakable news. That's her, that's them. No need to worry anymore, it is finished, you are free. No one could help these people who were weary of waiting and sick of hope like Jack could.

Miriam had a fondness for people who vanished, though she had never known any personally. But if she had a loved one who vanished, she would prefer to believe that they had fallen in love with distance, a great distance. She certainly wouldn't long to be told they were dead.

One day, one of Jack's students, an ardent hunter, a gangly blue-eyed boy named Carl who wore camouflage pants and a black shirt winter and summer, presented him with four cured deer feet. "I thought you'd like to make a lamp," Carl said.

Miriam was in the garden. She had taken to stealing distressed plants from nurseries and people's yards and planting them in an unused corner of the lot, far from Jack's roses. They remained distressed, however—in shock, she felt.

"It would make a nice lamp," Carl said. "You can make all kinds of things. With a big buck's forelegs you can make an outdoor thermometer. Looks good with snowflakes on it."

"A lamp," Jack said. He appeared delighted. Jack got along well with his students. He didn't sleep with the girls and he treated the boys as equals. He put his hands around the tops of the deer feet and splayed them out some.

"You might want to fiddle around with the height," Carl said. "You can make great stuff with antlers, too. Chandeliers, candelabras. You can use antlers to frame just about anything."

"We have lamps," Miriam said. She was holding a wan perennial she had liberated from a supermarket.

"Gosh, this appeals to me, though, Miriam."

"I bet you'd be good at this sort of thing, sir," Carl said. "I did one once and it was very relaxing." He glanced at Miriam, squeezed his eyes almost shut and smiled.

"It will be a novelty item, all right," Jack said. "I think it will be fun."

"Maybe you'd like to go hunting sometime with me, sir," Carl said. "We could go bowhunting for mulies together."

"You should resist the urge to do this, Jack, really," Miriam said. The thought of a lamp made of animal legs in her life and *turned on* caused a violent feeling of panic within her.

But Jack wanted to make a lamp. He needed another hobby, he argued. Hobbies were healthy, and he might even take Carl up on his bowhunting offer. Why didn't she get herself a hobby like baking or watching football, he suggested. He finished the lamp in a weekend and set it on an antique jelly cabinet in the sunroom. He'd had a little trouble trimming the legs to the same height. They might not have ended up being exactly the same height. Miriam, expecting to be repulsed by the thing, was enthralled instead. It had a dark blue shade and a gold-colored cord and a sixty-watt bulb. A brighter bulb would be pushing it, Jack said. Miriam could not resist the allure of the little lamp. She often found herself sitting beside it, staring at it, the harsh brown hairs, the dainty pasterns, the polished black hooves, all fastened together with a brass gimp band in a space the size of a dinner plate. It was anarchy, the little lamp, its legs snugly bunched. It was whirl, it was hole, it was the first far drums. She sometimes worried that she would begin talking to it. This happened to some people, she knew, they felt they had to talk. She read that Luther Burbank spoke to cactus reassuringly when he wanted to create a spineless variety and that they stabbed him repeatedly; he had to pull thousands of spines from his hands but didn't care. He continued to speak calmly and patiently; he never got mad, he persisted.

"Miriam," Jack said, "that is not meant to be a reading light. It's an accent light. You're going to ruin your eyes."

Miriam had once channeled her considerable imagination into sex, which Jack had long appreciated, but now it spilled everywhere and lay lightly on everything like water on a lake. It alarmed him a little. Perhaps, during semester break, they should take a trip together. To witness something strange with each other might be just the ticket. At the same time, he felt unaccountably nervous about traveling with Miriam.

The days were radiant but it was almost fall and a daytime coolness reached out and touched everything. Miriam's restlessness was gone. It was Jack who was restless.

"I'm going to take up bowhunting, Miriam," he said. "Carl seems to think I'd be a natural at it."

Miriam did not object to this as she might once have. Nevertheless, she could not keep herself from waiting anxiously beside the lamp for Jack's return from his excursions with Carl. She was in a peculiar sort of readiness, and not for anything in particular, either. For weeks Jack went hunting, and for weeks he did not mind that he did not return with a former animal.

"It's the expectation and the challenge. That's what counts," he said. He and Carl would stand in the kitchen sharing a little whiskey. Carl's skin was clean as a baby's and he smelled cleanly if somewhat aberrantly of cold cream and celery. "The season's young, sir," he said.

But eventually Jack's lack of success began to vex him. Miriam and the lamp continued to wait solemnly for his empty-handed return. He grew irritable. Sometimes he would forget to wash off his camouflage paint, and he slept poorly. Then, late one afternoon when Jack was out in the woods, he fell asleep in his stand and toppled out of a tree, critically wounding himself with his own arrow, which passed through his eye and into his head like a knife thrust into a cantaloupe. A large portion of his brain lost its rosy hue and turned gray as a rodent's coat. A month later, he could walk with difficulty and move one arm. He had some vision out of his remaining eye and he could hear but not speak. He emerged from rehab with a face expressionless as a frosted cake. He was something that had suffered a premature burial, something accounted for but not present. Miriam was certain that he was aware of the morbid irony in this.

The lamp was a great comfort to Miriam in the weeks following the accident. Carl was of less comfort. Whenever she saw him in the hospital's halls, he was wailing and grinding his teeth. But the crooked, dainty deer-foot lamp was calm. They spent most nights together quietly reading. The lamp had eclectic reading tastes. It would cast its light on anything, actually. It liked the stories of Poe. The night before Jack was to return home, they read a little book in which animals offered their prayers to God—the mouse, the bear, the turtle and so on—and this is perhaps where the lamp and Miriam had their first disagreement. Miriam liked the little verses. But the lamp felt that though the author clearly meant well, the prayers were cloying and confused thought with existence. The lamp had witnessed a smattering of Kierkegaard and felt strongly that thought should never be confused with existence. Being in such a condition of peculiar and altered existence itself, the lamp felt some things unequivocally. Miriam often wanted to think about that other life, when the parts knew the whole, when the legs ran and rested and moved through woods washed by flowers, but the lamp did not want to reflect upon those times.

Jack came back and Carl moved in with them. He had sold everything he owned except his big Chevy truck and wanted only to nurse Jack for the rest of his life. Jack's good eye often teared, and he indicated both discomfort and agreement with a whistling hiss. Even so, he didn't seem all that glad to see Miriam. As for herself, she felt that she had driven to a grave and gotten out of the car but left the engine running. Carl slept for a time in Jack's study, but one night when Miriam couldn't sleep and was sitting in the living room with the lamp, she saw him go into their room and shut the door. And that became the arrangement. Carl stayed with Jack day and night.

One of the first things Carl wanted to do was to take a trip. He believed that the doleful visits from the other students tired Jack and that the familiar house and grounds didn't stimulate him properly. Miriam didn't think highly of Carl's ideas but this one didn't seem too bad. She was ready to leave. After all, Jack had already left in his fashion and it seemed pointless to stay in his house. They all three would sit together in the big roomy cab on the wide cherry-red custom seat of Carl's truck and tour the Southwest. The only thing she didn't like was that the lamp would have to travel in the back with the luggage.

"Nothing's going to happen to it," Carl said. "Look at dogs. Dogs ride around in the backs of trucks all the time. They love it."

"Thousands of dogs die each year from being pitched out of the backs of pickups," Miriam said.

Jack remained in the room with them while they debated the statistical probability of this. He was gaunt and his head was scarred, and he tended to resemble, if left to his own devices, a large white appliance. But Carl was always buying him things and making small alterations to his appearance. This day he was wearing pressed khakis, a crisp madras shirt, big black glasses and a black Stetson hat. Carl was young and guilty and crazy in love. He patted Jack's wrists as he talked, not wanting to upset him.

Finally, continuing to assert that he had never heard of a dog falling out of a pickup truck, Carl agreed to buy a camper shell and enclose the back. He packed two small bags for himself and Jack while Miriam got a cardboard carton and arranged her clothes around the lamp. Her plan was to unplug whatever lamp was in whatever motel room they stayed in and plug in the deer-foot lamp. Clearly, this would be the high point of each day for it.

They took to the road that night and didn't stop driving until daylight disclosed that the landscape had changed considerably. There was a great deal of broken glass and huge cactus everywhere. Organ-pipe, saguaro, barrel cactus and prickly pear. Strange and stern shapes, far stiller than trees, less friendly and willing to serve. They seemed to be waiting for further transition, another awesome shift of the earth's plates, an enormous occurrence. The sun bathed each spine, it sharpened the smashed bottles and threw itself through the large delicate ears of car-crushed jackrabbits. They saw few people and no animals except dead ones. The land was vast and still and there seemed to be considerable resentment toward the nonhuman creatures who struggled to inhabit it. Dead coyotes and hawks were nailed to fence posts and the road was hammered with the remains of lizards and snakes. Miriam was glad that the lamp was covered and did not have to suffer these sights.

The first night they stopped at a motel, with a Chinese restaurant and lounge adjoining. Miriam ordered *moo goo gai pan* for dinner, something she had not had since she was a child, and an orange soda. Carl fed Jack some select tidbits from an appetizer platter with a pair of chopsticks. After they ate Miriam wandered into the lounge, but there was only a cat vigorously cleaning itself who stared at her with its legs splayed over its head. She picked up a couple of worn paperback books from the exchange table in the office and went back to her room. Through the walls she could hear Carl singing to Jack as he ran the bathwater. He would shampoo Jack's hair, scrub his nails and talk about the future . . . Miriam turned on the lamp and examined one of the books. It concerned desert plants but many of the pages were missing and someone had spilled wine on the pictures. She did learn, however, that cactus are descended from roses. They were late arrivals, adaptors, part of a new climate. She felt like that, felt very much a late arrival, it was her personality. She had adapted readily to being in love, and then adapted to not being in love anymore. And the new climate was, well, this situation. She put the book about cactus down.

The other book was about hunting zebras in Africa. *I shot him right up his big fat fanny,* the writer wrote. She had read this before she knew what she was doing and felt terrible about it, but the lamp held steady until she finally turned it off and got into bed.

The next day they drove. They stopped at hot springs and ghost towns. They stopped on an Indian reservation and Carl bought Jack colored sand in a bottle. They stopped at a Dairy Queen and Miriam drove while Carl spooned blueberry blizzard into Jack's mouth. They admired the desert, the peculiar growths, the odd pale colors. They passed through a canyon of large, solitary boulders. There was a sign threatening fine and imprisonment for defacing the rocks but the boulders were covered with paint, spelling out people's names, mostly. The shapes of the rocks resembled nothing but the words made them look like toilet doors in a truck stop. On the other side of the canyon was a small town with two museums, a brick hotel, a gas station and a large bar called the Horny Toad. Miriam had the feeling that the truck's engine had stopped running.

"Truck's stopped," Carl said.

They coasted to the side of the road and Carl fiddled with the ignition.

"Alternator's shot, I bet," he said. He took Jack's sunglasses off, wiped them with a handkerchief and carefully hooked them back over Jack's ears. He was thinking, Miriam thought. Underneath her elbow, the metal of the door was heating up.

"You check into the motel," Carl directed her. "Jack and I will walk down to the garage. He likes garages."

Carl helped Miriam get their luggage from the back and carried it into the hotel's lobby. She arranged for two unadjoining rooms. They were the last rooms left, even though the hotel and town appeared deserted. The museums were closed and everyone was at the bar, the manager told her. One of the museums displayed only a petrified wedding cake, a petrified cat, some rocks and old clothes. It was typical and not worth going into, the manager confided. But people came from far and wide to see the other museum and speak to the taxidermist on duty. He was surprised that they had come here without having the museum as their destination. The taxidermist was a genius. He couldn't make an animal look dead if he wanted to.

"He can even do reptiles and combine them in artistic and instructive groups," the manager said.

"This museum is full of dead animals?" Miriam said.

"Sure," the manager said. "It's a wildlife museum."

Miriam's room was in the back of the hotel over the kitchen and smelled like the inside of a lunch box, but it wasn't unpleasant. She rearranged the furniture, plugged in the lamp and gazed out the single window at the bar, a long, dark structure that seemed, the longer she stared at it, to be almost heaving with the muffled sound of voices. This was the Horny Toad. She decided to go there.

Miriam had always felt that she was the kind of person who somehow quenched in the least exacting stranger any desire for conversation with her. This, however, was not the case at the Toad. People turned to her immediately and began to speak. They had bright, restless faces, seemed starved for affection and were in full conversational mode. There were a number of children present. Everyone was wildly stimulated.

A young woman with lank, thinning hair touched Miriam with a small dry hand. "I'm Priscilla Dickman and I'm an ex-agoraphobic," she said. "Can I buy you a drink?"

"Yes," Miriam said, startled. People were waving, smiling.

"I used to be so afraid of losing control," Priscilla said. "I was afraid of going insane, embarrassing myself. I was afraid of getting sick or doing something frightening or dying. It's hard to believe, isn't it?"

She went off to the bar, saying she would return with gimlets. Miriam was immediately joined by an elderly couple wearing jeans, satin shirts and large, identical concha belts. Their names were Vern and Irene. They had spent all day at the museum and were happy and tired.

"My favorite is the javelina family," Irene said. "Those babies were adorable."

"Ugly animals," Vern said. "Bizarre. But they've always been Irene's favorite."

"Not last year," Irene said. "Last year it was the bears, I think. Vern says that Life is just one thing but it takes different forms to amuse itself."

"That's what I say, but I don't believe it," Vern said, winking broadly at Miriam.

"Vern likes the ground squirrels."

Vern agreed. "Isn't much of a display, but I like what I hear about them. That state-of-torpor thing. When the going gets rough, boom, right into a state of torpor. They don't need anything. A single breath every three minutes."

Irene didn't seem as fascinated as her husband by the state of torpor. "Have you gone yet, dear?" she asked Miriam. "Have you asked the taxidermist your question?"

"No, I haven't," Miriam said. She accepted a glass from Priscilla, who had returned with a tray of drinks. "I'm Priscilla Dickman," she said to the old couple, "and I'm an exagoraphobic."

"He doesn't answer everybody," Vern said.

"He answers the children sometimes, but they don't know what they're saying," Irene said fretfully. "I think children should be allowed only in the petting zoo."

A gaunt, grave boy named Alec arrived and identified himself as a tree-hugger. He was with a girl named Argon.

"When I got old enough to know sort of what I wanted?" Argon said, "I decided I wanted either a tree-hugger or a car guy. I'd narrowed it down to that. At my first demonstration, I lay in the road with some other people in a park where they were going to bulldoze two-hundred-year-old trees for a picnic area. We had attracted quite a crowd of onlooking picnickers. When the cops came and carried me off, a little girl said, 'Why are they taking away the pretty one, Mommy?' and I was hooked. I just loved demonstrating after that, always hoping to overhear those words again. But I never did."

"We all get older, dear," Irene said.

"Car guys are kind of interesting," Argon said. "They can be really hypnotic, but only when they're talking about cars, actually."

Sometime later, Alec was still in the midst of a long story about Indian environmentalists in the Himalayas. The tree-hugging movement started long ago, he'd been telling them, when the maharaja of Jodhpur wanted to cut down trees for yet another palace and a woman named Amrita Devi resisted his axmen by hugging a tree and uttering the now well-known phrase "A chopped head is cheaper than a felled tree" before she was dismembered. Then her three daughters took her place and they, too, were dismembered. Then three hundred and fifty-nine additional villagers were dismembered before the maharaja called it off.

"And it really worked," Alec said, gnawing on his thumb-nail. "That whole area is full of militant conservationists now. They have a fair there every year." He gnawed furiously at his nail. "And on the supposed spot where the first lady died, no grass grows. Not a single blade. They've got it cordoned off." He struggled for a moment with a piece of separated nail between his teeth, at last freed it, examined it for a moment, then flicked it to the floor.

"You know, Alec," Argon said, "I've never liked that story. It just misses the mark as far as I'm concerned." She turned to Miriam. "Tree-huggers tend sometimes not to have both feet on the ground. I want to be a spiritual and ecological warrior but I want both feet on the ground too."

Miriam looked at the white curving nail on the dirty floor. Jack wouldn't have had much to go on with that. Even Jack. Who were these people? They were all so desperate. You couldn't attribute their behavior to alcohol alone.

Other people gathered around the table, all talking about their experiences in the museum, all expressing awe at the exhibits, the mountain lions, the wading birds, the herds of elk and the exotics, particularly the exotics. They had come from far away to see this. Many of them returned, year after year.

"It's impossible to leave the place unmoved," a woman said.

"My favorite is the wood ibis on a stump in a lonely swamp," Priscilla said cautiously. "It couldn't be more properly delineated."

"That's a gorgeous specimen, all right. Not too many of those left," someone said.

". . . so much better than a zoo. Zoos are so depressing. I

hear the animals are committing suicide in Detroit. Hurling themselves into moats and drowning."

"I don't think other cities have that problem so much. Just Detroit."

"Even so. Zoos—"

"Oh, absolutely, this is so much nicer."

"Shoot to kill but not to mangle," Vern said.

"A lot of hunters just can't get that part down," Irene said. "And then they think they can bring those creatures here! To him!"

"I have my questions all prepared for tomorrow," Argon said. "I'm going to ask him about the eyes. Where do you get the eyes, I'm going to ask."

"A child got there ahead of you on that one, I'm afraid," Irene said. "Some little Goldilocks in a baseball hat."

"Oh, no!" Argon exclaimed. "What did he say?"

"He said he got the eyes from a supply house."

"I'm sure he would have expressed it differently to me," Argon said.

Alec, gnawing on his other thumb, looked helplessly at her.

"I just hate that," somebody said. "Someone else gets to ask your question, and you never get to the bottom of it."

"Excuse me," Miriam said quietly to Irene, "but why are you all here?"

"We're here with those we love because something big is going to happen here, we think," Irene said. "We want to be here for it. Then we'll have been here."

"You never know," Vern said. "Next year at this time, we might all have ridden over the skyline."

"But we're not ready to ride over the skyline yet," Irene said, patting his hand.

The lights in the Toad flickered, went out, then came back on again more weakly.

"It's closing time," several people said at once.

They all filed out into the night. Many were staying in campers and tents pitched around the museum, while others were staying in the hotel.

"I wouldn't want to pass my days in Detroit either," a voice said.

"I was using terror as an analgesic," Priscilla was explaining to no one, as far as Miriam could see. "And now I'm not."

Argon was yelling at Alec, "But your life's center is on the periphery."

Back in the room, Miriam sat with the lamp for some time. The legs were dusty so she wiped them down with a damp towel. She was thinking of getting different shades for it. Shade of the week. Even if she slurred her words when she thought, the lamp was able to follow her. There were tenses that human speech had yet to discover, and the lamp was able to incorporate these in its understanding as well. Miriam was excited about going to the museum in the morning. She planned on being there the moment the doors opened. The lamp had no interest in seeing the taxidermist. It was beyond that. They read a short, sad story about a brown dog whose faith in his master proved to be terribly misplaced, and spent a rather fitful night.

The next morning Miriam joined Jack and Carl in their room for breakfast.

"We've just finished brushing our teeth," Carl said. Jack's glasses were off and he regarded Miriam skittishly out of his good eye. She poured the coffee while Carl buttered the toast and Jack peeled the backing off Band-Aids and stuck them on things. He preferred children's adhesive bandages with space-ships and cartoon characters on them to the flesh-colored ones. He plastered some on Miriam's hands.

"He likes you!" Carl exclaimed.

They drank their coffee in silence. A fan whined in the room.

"Truck should be ready today," Carl said.

"Have you ever been in love before?" Miriam asked him.

"No," Carl said.

"Well, you're handling it very well, I think."

"No problem," Carl said.

Miriam held her cup. She pretended there was one more sip in it when there wasn't. "Why don't we all go to the museum," she said. "That's what people do when they're here."

"I've heard about that," Carl said. "And I would say that a museum like that, and the people who run it—well, it's deeply into denial on every level. That's what I'd say. And Jack here, all his life he was the great verifier—weren't you, Jack? And still are, by golly." Jack cleared his throat and Carl gazed at him happily. "We don't want to go into a place like that," Carl said.

Miriam felt ashamed and determined. "I'll go over there for just an hour or two," she said.

There were many people in line ahead of her, although she didn't see any of her acquaintances of the night before. The museum was massive with wide cement columns and curving walls of tinted glass. She could dimly make out static, shaggy arrangements within. The first room she entered was a replica of a famous basketball player's den in California. There were 1,500 wolf muzzles on the wall. A small bronze tablet said that Wilt Chamberlain had bought a whole year's worth of wolves from an Alaskan bounty hunter. It said he wanted the room to have an unequivocally masculine look. Miriam heard one man say hoarsely to another, "He got that, by god." The next few rooms were reproductions of big-game hunters' studies and were full of heads and horns and antlers. In the restaurant, a group of giraffes were arranged behind the tables as though in the act of chewing grass, the large lashed eyes in their angular Victorian faces content. In the petting area, children toddled among the animals, pulling their tails and shaking their paws. Miriam stepped quickly past flocks and herds and prides of creatures to stand in a glaring space before a polar bear and two cubs.

"Say hi to the polar bear," a man said to his child.

"Hi!" the child said.

"She's protecting her newborn cubs, that's why she's snarling like that," the man said.

"It's dead," Miriam remarked. "The whole little family."

"Hi, polar bear," the child crooned. "Hi, hi, hi."

"What's the matter with you?" the father demanded of Miriam. "People like you make me sick."

Miriam threw out her hand and slapped his jaw. He dropped the child's hand and she slapped him again even harder, then hurried from the room.

She wandered among the crowds. The museum was lit dimly and flute music played. The effect was that of a funeral parlor or a dignified cocktail lounge. All the animals were arranged in a state of extreme and hopeless awareness. Wings raised, jaws open, hindquarters bunched. All recaptured from death to appear at the brink of departure.

"They're glorious, aren't they?" a woman exclaimed.

"Tasteful," someone said.

"None of these animals died a natural death, though," a pale young man said. "That's what troubles me a little."

"These are trophy animals," his companion said. "It would be unnatural for them to die a natural death. It would be disgusting. It would be like Marilyn Monroe or something. James Dean, for example."

"It troubled me just a little. I'm all right now."

"That's not the way things work, honey," his companion said.

Miriam threaded her way past a line of people waiting to see the taxidermist. He was seated in a glass room. Beside him was a small locked room filled with skins and false bodies. There were all kinds of shapes, white and smooth.

The taxidermist sat behind a desk on which there were various tools—scissors and forceps, calipers and stuffing rods. A tiny, brilliantly colored bird lay on a blotter. Behind the taxidermist was a large nonhuman shape on which progress appeared to have slowed. It looked as though it had been in this stage of the process for a long time. The taxidermist was listening to a question that was being asked.

"I'm a poet," a man with a shovel-shaped face said, "and I recently accompanied two ornithologists into the jungles of Peru to discover heretofore unknown birds. I found the process of finding, collecting, identifying, examining and skinning hundreds of specimens for use in taxonomic studies tedious. I became disappointed. In other words, I found the labor of turning rare birds into specimens mundane. Isn't your work a bit mundane as well?"

"You're mundane," the taxidermist said. His voice was loud

and seemed to possess a lot of chilled space around it. It was like an astronaut's voice.

He fixed his eyes on Miriam, then waved and gestured to her. The gesture indicated that he wanted her to come around to the side of the glass room. He pulled down a long black shade on which were the words *The Taxidermist Will Be Right Back.*

"I saw and heard everything back there," he said to Miriam. "There are monitors and microphones all over this place. I like a woman with spirit. I find that beliefs about reality affect people's actions to an enormous degree, don't you? Have you read Marguerite Porete's *Mirror of Simple Annihilated Souls?*"

Miriam shook her head. It sounded like something the lamp would like. She would try to acquire it.

"Really? I'm surprised. Well-known broad. She was burned at the stake, but an enormous crowd was converted to her favor after witnessing her attitude toward death."

"What was her attitude?" Miriam said.

"I don't know exactly. Thirteenth century. The records are muzzy. I guess she went out without a lot of racket about it. Women have been trying to figure out how to be strong for a long while. It's harder for a woman to find a way than it is for a man. Not crying about stuff doesn't seem to be enough."

Miriam said nothing. Back in the room, the lamp was hovered over *Moby-Dick*. It would be deeply involved in it by now. It would be slamming down Melville like water. The shapeless maw of the undifferentiating sea! God as indifferent, insentient Being, composed of an infinitude of deaths! Nature.

Gliding . . . bewitching . . . majestic . . . capable of universal catastrophe! The lamp was eating it up.

"I've been here for ten years," the taxidermist said. "I built this place up from nothing. The guy before me had nothing but a few ratty displays. Medallions were his specialty. Things have to look dead on a medallion, that's the whole point. But when I finished with something it looked alive. You could almost hear it breathe. But of course it wasn't breathing. Ha! It was best when I was working on it, that's when it really existed, but when I stopped . . . uhhh," he said. "I've done as much as I can. I've reached my oubliette. Do you know what I'm saying?"

"I do," Miriam said.

"Oh," he said, "I'm crazy about that word *oubliette*. That word says it all."

"It's true," she said.

"You're perfect," he said. "I want to retire, and I want you to take my place."

"I couldn't possibly," Miriam said.

"No stuffing would be required. I've done all that, we're beyond that. You'd just be answering questions."

"I don't know anything about questions," Miriam said.

"The only thing you have to know is that you can answer them anyway you want. The questions are pretty much the same, so you'll go nuts if you don't change the answers."

"I'll think about it," Miriam said. But actually she was thinking about the lamp. The odd thing was she had never been in love with an animal. She had just skipped that cross-species eroticism and gone right beyond it to altered parts. There was something wrong with that, she thought. It was so hopeless. Well, love was hopeless . . .

"I have certain responsibilities," Miriam said. "I have a lamp."

"That's a wonderful touch!" the taxidermist said. "And when things are slow you'll have all the animals too. There are over a thousand of them here, you know, and some of them are pretty darn rare. I think you'll be making up lots of stories about them."

It seemed a pretty good arrangement for the lamp. Miriam made up her mind. "All right," she said.

"You'll have a following in no time," the taxidermist said. "I'll finish up with these people and you can start in the morning."

There was still a long line of people waiting to get into the museum. Miriam passed them on her way out.

"I've been back five times," a bald woman was saying to her friend. "I think you'll find it's almost a quasi-religious experience."

"Oh, I think everything should be like that," her friend said.

Carl's big truck was no longer at the garage. Miriam gazed around but the truck did not resume its appearance and probably, as far as she was concerned, never would. For most people, and apparently Carl and Jack were two of them, a breakdown meant that it was just a matter of time before they were back on the road again. She walked over to the hotel and up the stairs to their room. The door was open and the beds were stripped. The big pillows without their pretty covers looked like flayed things. A thin maid in a pink uniform was changing the channel on a television set. Something was being described by the announcer as *a plume of effluent surrounded by seagulls* . . .

45

The maid noticed her and said, "San Diego, a sewer pipe broke. A single pipe for one-point-four-million people. A million-four, what do they expect."

Miriam continued down the corridor and opened the door quietly to her own room. She looked at the lamp. The lamp looked back, looked at her as though it had no idea who she was. Miriam knew that look. She'd always felt it was full of promise. Nothing could happen anywhere was the truth of it. And the lamp was burning with this. Burning!

MARABOU

THE FUNERAL of Anne's son, Harry, had not gone smoothly. Other burials were taking place at the same hour, including that of a popular singer several hundred yards away whose mourner fans carried on loudly under a lurid striped tent. Still more fans pressed against the cemetery's wrought-iron gates, screaming and eating potato chips. Anne had been distracted. She gazed at the other service in disbelief, thinking of the singer's songs that she had heard now and then on the radio.

Her own group, Harry's friends, was subdued. They were pale, young, and all wore sunglasses. Most of them were classmates from the prep school he had graduated from two years before, and all were addicts, or former addicts of some sort. Anne couldn't tell the difference between those who were recovering and those who were still hard at it. She was sure there was a difference, of course, and it only appeared there wasn't. They all had a manner. There were about twenty of them, boys and girls, strikingly alike in black. Later she took them all out to a restaurant. "Death . . . by none art thou understood," one boy kept saying. "Henry Vaughan."

They were all bright enough, Anne supposed. After a while he stopped saying it. They had calamari, duck, champagne, everything. They were on the second floor of the restaurant and had the place to themselves. They stayed for hours. By the time they left, one girl was saying earnestly, "You know a word I like is *interplanetary.*"

Then she brought them back to the house, although she locked Harry's rooms. Young people were sentimentalists, consumers. She didn't want them carrying off Harry's things, his ties and tapes, anything at all. They sat in the kitchen. They were beginning to act a little peculiar, Anne thought. They didn't talk about Harry much, though one of them remembered a time when Harry was driving and he stopped at all the green lights and proceeded on the red. They all acted as though they'd been there. This seemed a fine thing to remember about Harry. Then someone, a floppy-haired boy who looked frightened, remembered something else, but it turned out this was associated with a boy named Pete who was not even present.

At about one o'clock in the morning, Anne said that when she and Harry were in Africa, during the very first evening at the hotel in Victoria Falls, he claimed he'd seen a pangolin, a peculiar anteater-like animal. He described it, and that's clearly what it was, but a very rare thing, an impossible thing for him to have seen, really, and no one in the group they would be traveling with believed him. He had been wandering around the hotel grounds by himself, so there were no witnesses to it. The group went on to discuss the falls. Everyone could verify the impression the falls made. So many hundreds of millions of gallons of water went over each minute or something, and there was a drop of four hundred feet. Even so, everyone was quite aware it wasn't like that, no one was satisfied with that. The sound of the falls was like silence, total amplified silence, the sight of it exclusionary. And all that could be done was to look at it, this astonishing thing, Victoria Falls, then eventually stop looking and go on to something else.

The next day Harry had distinguished himself further by exclaiming over a marabou stork, and someone in the group told him that marabous were gruesome things, scavengers, "morbidity distilled," in the words of this fussy little person, and certainly nothing to get excited about when there were hundreds of beautiful and strange creatures in Africa that one could enjoy and identify and point out to the others. Imagine, Anne said, going to an immense new continent and being corrected as to one's feelings, one's perceptions, in such a strange place. And it was not as though everything was known. Take the wild dogs, for example. Attitudes had changed utterly about the worth of wild dogs . . .

Abruptly, she stopped. She had been silent much of the evening and felt that this outburst had not gone over particularly well. Harry's friends were making margaritas. One of them had gone out and just returned with more tequila. They were watching her uncomfortably, as though they felt she should fluff up her stories on Harry a bit.

Finally one of them said, "I didn't know Harry had been to Africa."

This surprised her. The trip to Africa hadn't been a triumph, exactly, but it hadn't been a disaster either and could very well have been worse. They had been gone a month, and this had been very recently. But it didn't matter. She would probably never see these children again.

They sat around the large kitchen. They were becoming more and more strange to her. She wondered what they were all waiting for. One of them was trying to find salt. Was there no salt? He opened a cupboard and peered inside, bringing out a novelty set, a plastic couple, Amish or something; she supposed the man was pepper, the woman salt. They were all watching him as he turned the things over and shook them against his cupped hand. Anne never cooked, never used anything in this kitchen, she and Harry ate out, so these things were barely familiar to her. Then, with what was really quite a normal gesture, the boy unscrewed the head off the little woman and poured the salt inside onto a saucer.

Someone shrieked in terror. It was the floppy-haired boy; he was yelling, horrified. Anne was confused for an instant. Was Harry dying again? Was Harry all right? The boy was howling, his eyes rolling in his head. The others looked at him dully. One of the girls giggled. "Uh-oh," she said.

Two of the boys were trying to quiet him. They all looked like Harry, even the boy who was screaming.

"You'd better take him to the emergency room," Anne said.

"Maybe if he just gets a little air, walks around, gets some air," a boy said.

"You'd all better go now," Anne said.

. . .

It was not yet dawn, still very dark. Anne sat there alone in the bright kitchen in her black dress. There was a run in her stocking. The dinner in the restaurant had cost almost a thousand dollars, and Harry probably wouldn't even have liked it. She hadn't liked it. She wanted to behave differently now, for

Harry's sake. He hadn't been perfect, Harry, he'd been a very troubled boy, a very misunderstood boy, but she had never let him go, never, until now. She knew that he couldn't be aware of that, that she now had let him go. She knew that between them, from now on, she alone would be the one who realized things. She wasn't going to deceive herself in that regard. Even so, she knew she wasn't thinking clearly about this.

After some time, she got up and packed a duffel bag for Africa, exactly the way she had done before. The bag and its contents could weigh no more than twenty-two pounds. When she was finished, she put it in the hallway by the door. Outside it was still dark, as dark as it had been hours ago, though this scarcely seemed possible.

Perhaps she would go back to Africa.

There was a knock on the door. Anne looked at it, startled, a thick door with locks. Then she opened it. A girl was standing there, not the *interplanetary* one but another, one who had particularly relished the dinner. She had been standing there smoking for a while before she knocked. Several cigarette butts were ground into the high-gloss cerulean of the porch.

"May I come in?" the girl asked.

"Why, no," Anne said. "No, you may not."

"Please," the girl said.

Anne shut the door.

She went into the kitchen and threw the two parts of the salt shaker into the trash. She tossed the small lady's companion in as well. Harry had once said to her, "Look, this is amazing, I don't know how this could have happened but I have these spikes in my head. They must have been there for a while, but I swear, I swear to you, I just noticed them. But I got them out! On the left side. But on the right side it's more difficult because they're in a sort of helmet, and the helmet is fused to my head, see? Can you help me?"

She had helped him then. She had stroked his hair with her fingers for a long, long time. She had been very careful, very thorough. But that had been a unique situation. Usually, she couldn't help him.

There was a sound at the door again, a determined knocking. Anne walked to it quickly and opened it. There were several of Harry's friends there, not just the girl but not all of them either.

"You don't have to be so rude," one of them said.

They were angry. They had lost Harry, she thought, and they missed him.

"We loved Harry too, you know," one of them said. His tie was loose, and his breath was sweet and dry, like sand.

"I want to rest now," Anne said. "I must get some rest."

"Rest," one of them said in a soft, scornful voice. He glanced at the others. They ignored him.

"Tell us another story about Harry," one of them said. "We didn't get the first one."

"Are you frightening me?" Anne said. She smiled. "I mean, are you trying to frighten me?"

"I think Harry saw that thing, but I don't think he was ever there. Is that what you meant?" one of them said with some effort. He turned and then, as though he were dancing, moved down the steps and knelt on the ground, where he lowered his head and began spitting up quietly.

"Harry will always be us," one of them said. "You better get used to it. You better get your stories straight."

"Good night," Anne said.

"Good night, *please,*" they said, and Anne shut the door.

She turned off all the lights and sat in the darkness of her house. Before long, as she knew it would, the phone began to ring. It rang and rang, but she didn't have to answer it. She wouldn't do it. It would never be that once, again, when she'd learned that Harry died, no matter how much she knew in her heart that the present was but a past in that future to which it belonged, that the past, after all, couldn't be everything.

THE VISITING
PRIVILEGE

DONNA CAME AS a visitor in her long black coat. It was spring but still cool, and she never wore light colors, she was no buttercup. She was visiting her friend Cynthia, who was in Pond House for depression. Donna never had a drink before she visited Cynthia. She shunned her habitual excesses and arrived sober and aware, with an exquisite sinking feeling. She thought that Pond House was an unfortunate name, ponds being stagnant, artificial and small. This wasn't just her opinion. A pond was indeed an artificially confined body of water, she argued, but Cynthia thought Pond was probably the name of the hospital wing's benefactor. Cynthia had three roommates, a woman in her sixties and two obese teenagers. Donna liked to pretend that the old woman was her mother. Hi, she'd say, you look great today, what a pretty sweatshirt.

Donna had been visiting Cynthia for about a week now. She could scarcely imagine what she had done with herself before Cynthia had the grace to get herself committed to Pond House. She liked everything about it but she particularly liked sitting in Cynthia's room, speaking quietly with her while the others listened. They didn't even pretend not to listen, the others. But sometimes she and Cynthia would stroll down to the lounge and get a snack from the fridge. In the lounge, goofy helium balloons in the shape of objects or food but with human features were tied to the furniture with ribbon. They bobbed there opposite the nurse's station, and people would bat them as they passed by. Cynthia thought the balloons would be deeply disturbing to anyone who was already disturbed, yet in fact everyone considered them amusing. None of the people at Pond House were supposed to be seriously ill, at least on Floor Three. On Floor Four it was another matter. But here they were supposed to be sort of ruefully aware of their situations, and were encouraged to believe that they could possibly be helped. Cynthia had come here because she had picked up the habit of committing destructive and selfish acts, the most recent being the torching of·her boyfriend's car, a black Corvette. The boyfriend was married but Cynthia strongly suspected he was gay. He drove her crazy. "He's a taker and not a giver, Donna," she told Donna earnestly.

She said that she was so discouraged that everything seemed vaguely yellow to her, that she saw everything through a veil of yellow.

"That was in an article I read," Donna said excitedly. "The yellow part."·

"You know, Donna," Cynthia said, "you're part of my problem."

When Cynthia got like this, Donna would excuse herself

and go away for a while. Or she would go back to the room and talk with the old woman. She got a kick out of being extraordinarily friendly to her. Once she brought her gum, another time a jar of night cream. She ignored the obese teenagers, but one afternoon one of them deliberately bumped into her as she walked down the hall. The girl's flesh was hard and she smelled of coconut. She thrust her face close to Donna's. Her pores were large and clean and Donna could see the contacts resting on the corneas of her eyes.

"I'm passionate, intense and filled with private reverie, and so is my friend," the girl said, "so don't slime us like you do." Then she punched Donna viciously on the arm. Donna felt like crying but she was only a visitor. She didn't have to come here so frequently; she was really coming here too much, sometimes two and three times a day.

There were group meetings twice a week and Donna always tried to be present for these, although she was not permitted to attend them. Sometimes, however, if she stood just outside the door, the nurses and psychologists didn't notice her right away. Cynthia and the fat teenagers and the old lady and a half dozen others would sit around a large table and say anything they wanted to.

. . .

"I dreamed that I threw up a fox," one of the fat girls said. Really, Donna couldn't tell them apart.

"I shit something that looked like an onion once," a man said. "It just kept coming out of me. I pulled it out of myself with my own hands. I thought it was the Devil, but it was a worm. A gift from Central America."

"That is so disgusting," the other fat girl said, "That is the most—"

"Hey!" the man said. "Get yourself a life, woman."

The worm thing caused the old lady to request to be excused. Donna walked back to the room with her, and they sat down on her bed.

"Feel my heart," the old lady said. "It's pounding. I wasn't brought up that way."

The old lady liked to play cards, and she and Donna would often play with an old soiled deck that had pictures of colorful fish on it. Donna pretended she was in the cabin of a boat on a short, safe trip to a lovely island. The old woman was a mysterious opponent, not at all what she seemed. Donna had, in fact, been told by the nurses that she was considerably more impaired than she appeared to be. Beyond the window of the cabin were high waves, pursuing and accompanying them. The waves were an essential part of the world the boat required, but they bore malice toward the boat, that much was obvious.

"What kind of fish are these?" Donna asked.

"These are reef residents," the old lady said.

They played a variation of Spit in the Ocean. Donna had had no idea that there were so many variations of this humble game.

The two fat girls came in and lay down on their beds. The old lady was really opening up to Donna. She was telling her about her husband and her little house.

"After my husband died, I was afraid someone might come in and . . ." She passed her finger across her throat. "I bought one of those men. Safe-T-Man II, the New Generation. You know, the ones that look as though they're six feet tall but can be folded up and put in a little tote bag? I put him in the car or

I put him in my husband's easy chair right in front of the window. He had all kinds of clothes. He had a leather coat. He had a baseball cap."

"Where is he now?" Donna asked.

"He's in his little tote bag. Actually, he frightened me a little, Safe-T-Man. I think I ordered him too dark or something. I never did get used to him."

"That's racist," one of the fat girls said.

"Yeah, what a racist remark," the other one said.

"I bet he wonders what happened to me," the old lady said. "I bet my car does too. One minute you're on the open road, one excitement after another, the next you're in a dark garage. I'm not afraid of dying, but I don't want to die old."

She was quite old already, of course, but the fat girls did not challenge her on this. Cynthia came into the room, eating a piece of fruit, a nectarine or something.

"The first thing I'm going to do when I get out of here is go home and make Festive Chicken," the old woman said. "I hope you'll all be my guests for dinner."

The fat girls and Cynthia stared at her.

"I'd love to," Donna said. "What is Festive Chicken? Can I bring anything? Wine? A salad?"

"It requires toothpicks," the old woman said. "You bake it with toothpicks but then you take the toothpicks out."

"It sounds wonderful," Donna said.

Cynthia rolled her eyes. "Would you give it a rest," she said to Donna.

"I'm tired now," the old woman said sweetly. "I'm tired of playing cards." She put the cards back in the box but it didn't have reef residents on it. It had a picture of a drab, many-spired European city, the very opposite of a reef resident.

"These don't belong in this box!" she cried. "It's the first time I've noticed this. Would you go to my house and bring back the other deck of cards?" she asked Donna.

"Sure," Donna said.

"My house is a little strange," the old woman said.

"What do you mean?"

"I bet it is," one of the fat girls said.

"I love my little house," the old woman said anxiously. "I want to get back to it as soon as I can."

She gave Donna the address and a key from her pocketbook. That evening, when visiting hours were over, Donna drove to the house, which was boxy and tidy with a crushed-rock yard and a dead nestling in the driveway. The house didn't seem that strange to Donna. One would be desperate to get out of it, certainly. There were lots of things that were meant to be plugged into wall outlets but none of them were plugged in. She found the cards almost immediately, in the kitchen. There were the colorful fish on the cover of the box and the deck inside had the image of the foreign city. Idly, she opened the refrigerator, which was full of ketchup, nothing but bottles of ketchup, each one partially used. Donna had an urge to top the bottles up from others, to reduce the unseemly number, but with not much effort she resisted this.

On the way back to her apartment she stopped at a restaurant and had several drinks in the bar. The bartender's name was Lucy. She had just come back from a vacation. She had spent forty-five minutes swimming with dolphins. The dolphin that had persisted in keeping Lucy company had an immense boner.

"He kept gliding past me, gliding past," Lucy said, moving her hand through the air. "I kept worrying about the little kids.

They're always bringing in these little kids who have only weeks to live due to one thing or another. I would think it would be pretty undesirable for them to experience a dolphin with a boner."

"But the dolphins know better than that, don't they?" Donna said.

"It's not all that relaxing to swim with them, actually," the bartender said. "They like some people better than others, and the ones that get ignored feel like shit. You know, out of the Gaia loop."

People in the restaurant kept requesting exotic drinks that Lucy had to look up in her Bartender's Bible. After a while, Donna went home.

The next afternoon she swept into Pond House in her long black coat bearing a bunch of daffodils as a gift in general.

Cynthia was in the lounge in a big chintz slipcovered chair reading *Anna Karenina*.

"Should you be reading that?" Donna asked.

Cynthia wouldn't talk to her.

Donna found the old lady and gave her the deck of cards.

"I'm so relieved," the old lady said. "That could have been such a problem, such a problem. Would you do me another favor? Would you get my dog and bring him to me here?"

Donna was enthusiastic about this. "Do you have a dog? Where is he?"

"He's in my house."

"Is anyone feeding him?" Donna said. "Does he have water?" She had found her vocation, she was sure of it. She could do this forever. She felt like a long-distance swimmer in that place long-distance swimmers go in their heads when they're good.

"Nooooooo," the old woman said. "He doesn't need water." She, too, looked delighted. She and Donna beamed at each other. "He's a good dog, a watchdog."

"I didn't see him when I was there," Donna admitted.

"He wasn't watching you," the old lady said.

"What breed of dog is he?" Donna asked.

She suddenly looked concerned. "He's something you plug in."

"Oh," Donna said, disappointed. "I think I did notice him." He looked like a stereo speaker. She thought they'd been talking more along the lines of Cerberus, the dog that guarded the gates of hell. Those Greeks! It wasn't that you couldn't get in, it was that you couldn't get out. And that honeycake business . . . Actually, she had never grasped the honeycake business.

"He detects intruders up to thirty feet and he barks. He can detect them through glass, brick, wood and cement. The closer they get, the louder and faster he barks. He's just a little individual but he sounds ferocious. I always liked him better than Safe-T-Man. I got them at the same time."

"But he'd be barking all the time here," Donna said. "You have to consider that," she added.

"He can be quiet," the woman said. "He can be good."

"I'll get him for you then," Donna said as though she had just made a difficult decision.

As she was leaving Pond House she passed a man dressed all in red yelling into the telephone. There was a pay phone at the very heart of Floor Three and it was always in use. "What were you born with, an ax in your hand?" he shouted. "You're so destructive."

Donna returned the next day with the old lady's dog,

which she carried in a smart brown and white Bendel's shopping bag she'd been saving. She arrived just about the time the group meeting was coming to a close. Lingering near the door, she saw the fat teenagers and Cynthia's round neat head with its fashionable haircut. A male patient she had not seen before was saying, "Hey, if it looks, walks, talks, smells and feels like the anima, then it is the anima." Donna thought this very funny and somewhat obscene. "Miss!" someone called to her. "You are not allowed in these meetings!" She went back to Cynthia's room and sat on her bed. The old woman's bed was stripped down to the ticking. She sat and looked at it vacantly.

When Cynthia came in, she said, "Donna, that old lady died, honest to God. We were all sitting around after dinner eating our goddamn Jell-O and she just tipped over."

"I have something she wanted here," Donna said, raising the bag. "This is hers, it's from her house."

"Get rid of it," Cynthia said. "Listen, act quickly and positively." She began to cry.

Donna thought her friend's response somewhat peculiar, but that was probably why she was in Pond House.

As the day wore on, it was disclosed that the woman had no family. There was no one.

"There wouldn't have been any Festive Chicken either," Cynthia said, "that's for sure." She had her old mouth back on her, Donna noticed.

There was discussion in the room about what had happened. The old lady had been eating the Jell-O. She hadn't said a word. She'd expressed no dismay.

"She was clueless," one of the fat girls said.

"Were you friends before you came here or did you become friends here?" Donna asked them.

They looked at her with hatred. "She's a nut fucker, I think," one of them said.

They looked so much alike Donna couldn't be sure which of them had struck her in the hallway. She thought of them as Dum and Dee. She pretended she was a docent leading tours. The neuroses of these two, Dum and Dee, are so normal they're of little concern to us, she would say, indicating the fat girls. Then she pretended they were her jailers over whom she held indisputable moral sway.

The barking-dog alarm had not worked at the old lady's house. It was a simple enough thing, with few adjustments that could be made to it; its function would either be realized or it wouldn't, and it wasn't. Donna had gone outside into the street and walked slowly back toward the house, avoiding the nestling. Then she had run, waving her arms. There had been no barking at all, only the sound of her own feet on the crushed-rock yard. It had not worked in her own apartment either. It had not even felt warm.

Poor old soul, Donna thought.

Night was flickering at the corners of the hospital. There was the smell of potatoes, the sound of wheels bringing the supper trays. They always made the visitors leave around this time.

"Cynthia," Donna said. "I'll see you tomorrow."

"Why?" Cynthia said.

At home, Donna pretended she was on a train with no ticket, eluding the conductor as it sped toward some destination on gleaming rails. She made herself a drink. She almost finished it, then freshened it a bit. The phone rang and it was Cynthia. She was delighted it was Cynthia.

"You will not believe this, Donna," Cynthia said. "You know that new guy, the really annoying one? Well, at dinner he was saying that when women attempt suicide they often don't succeed, but with men they do it on the first go-round. He said that simple statistic says it all about the difference between men and women. He said that men are doers and that women are deceivers and flirts, and Holly just threw back her chair and—"

"Who's Holly?" Donna asked.

"My roommate, for godssakes, the one who hates you. She attacked this guy. She gouged out one of his eyes with a spoon."

"She gouged it *out?*"

"I didn't think it could be done, but boy, she knew how to do it."

"I wonder if that could have been me," Donna said.

"Oh, I think so. It's bedlam in here." Cynthia laughed wildly. "I want to leave, Donna, but I don't feel better. But I could leave, you know. I could just walk right out of here."

"Really?" Donna said. She thought, When I get out of here, I'm going to be gone.

"But I think I should feel better. I lack goals. I need goals."

Maybe it wasn't such a good idea, Cynthia using the phone. Donna preferred sitting quietly with her in Pond House, offering to get her little things she had expressed no desire for, reflecting about Dennis, her married man who had not come by to see her once. Of course he was probably still annoyed about his car, although he had filed no charges.

Cynthia kept talking, pretty much about her life, the details of which Donna had heard before and which were no more riveting this time. She'd had a difficult time of it, starting in childhood. She had been an intense little thing but was thwarted, thwarted. Donna walked around with the phone to her ear, making another drink, crushing an ant or two that ventured onto the countertop, staring out the window at the dark only to realize that she wasn't seeing the dark, merely a darkened image of herself and the objects behind her. She sipped her drink and turned toward some picture postcards she'd taped to one of the cupboards. Some of them had been up for years. One was of a city, a cheerless and civilized city similar to the one on the old woman's playing cards.

Cynthia was saying, "I just can't accept so much, you know, Donna, and I feel, I really feel this, that my capacity to adapt to what *is* has been exceeded. I—"

"Cynthia," Donna said. "We're all alone in a meaningless world. That's it. OK?"

"That's so easy for you to say!" Cynthia screamed.

There was a loud crack as the connection was broken.

Donna had no recollection who had sent her the postcard or from where. She couldn't think what had prompted her to display it, either. The city held no allure for her. She had no intention of taking it down and looking at it more closely.

Later, she lay in bed trying to find sleep by recounting the rank of poker hands. Royal Flush, Straight Flush, Four of a Kind, Full House . . . A voice kept saying in her head, *Out or In. Huh? Which will it be?* Then it was dawn. She had not slept but she felt alert, glassy even. She showered and dressed and hurried to Pond House, where she had coffee in the cafeteria. Her eyes darted about, falling on everything, glittering. There was her coat, hanging on a hook next to her table. The coat seemed preposterous to her suddenly. Honestly, what must she look like in that coat?

Up on Floor Three, Cynthia wasn't in her room but one fat girl was, her face red and her eyes swollen from crying.

"I just lost my friend," the fat girl said.

"You're not Holly then," Donna said.

"I wish I was," the fat girl said. "I wish I was Holly." She lay on her bed, crying loudly.

Donna looked out the window at the street below. You couldn't open the windows. A tree outside was struggling to burst into bloom but had been compromised heavily by the parking area. Big chunks of its bark had been torn away by poorly parked cars. When she was a child, visiting Florida, she'd seen a palm tree burst into flames. It was beautiful! Then rats as long as her downy child's arm had rushed down the trunk. Later, she learned that it was not unusual for a palm tree to do this on occasion, given the proper circumstances. This tree didn't want to do anything like that, though. It couldn't. It struggled along quietly.

She turned from the window and left the room where the fat girl continued sobbing. She walked down the corridor, humming a little. She pretended she was a virus, wandering without aim through someone's body. She found Cynthia in the lounge, painting her long and perfect nails.

Cynthia regarded her sourly. "I really wish you wouldn't visit me anymore," she said.

A nurse appeared from nowhere like they did, a new one. "Who are you visiting?" she said to Donna.

Cynthia looked at her little bottle of nail polish and tightened the cap.

"You have to be visiting someone," the nurse said.

"She's not visiting me," Cynthia muttered.

"What?" the nurse said.

"She's not visiting me," Cynthia said loudly.

After some remonstrance, Donna found herself being

steered away from Cynthia and down the hallway to the elevator. "That's it," the nurse said. "You've lost your privileges here." Donna was alone in the elevator as it went down. On the ground floor some people got on and the elevator went up again. On Floor Three they got off. Donna went back down. She walked through the parking lot to her car.

She would come back tomorrow and avoid Cynthia and the nurse, too. For now, she had to decide which route to take home. It was how they made roads these days; there were five or six ways to get to the same place. On the highway she ran into construction almost immediately. There was always construction. Cans and cones, those bright orange arrows blinking, and she had to merge. She inched over, trying to merge. They wouldn't let her in! She pushed her way in. Then she realized she was part of a funeral procession. Their lights were on. She was part of a cortège, of an anguished throng. Should she turn on her lights to show sympathy, to apologize? She put on her sunglasses. People didn't turn their lights on in broad daylight just for funerals, though. They turned them on for all sorts of things. Remembering somebody or something. Actually, showing you remembered somebody or something, which was different. People were urged to put them on for safety too. *Lights on for Safety*. But this was a funeral, no doubt about it.

After what seemed an eternity, the road opened up again and Donna turned the car sharply into the other lane. In quick moments she had left the procession far behind.

On her own street she parked and walked quickly toward her door. She felt an unpleasant excitement. It was midmorning, and as always the neighborhood was quiet. Who knew what people did here? She never saw anyone on this street.

Then a dog began to bark, quite alarmingly. As she walked

on, the rapid cry grew louder, more frantic. It was the poor old soul's dog, Donna thought, the gray machine, somehow operative again, resuming its purpose. She *knew*. But it sounded so real, so remarkably real, and the disorder she felt was so remarkably real as well that she hesitated. She could not go forward. Then, she couldn't go back.

SUBSTANCE

WALTER GOT THE SILK pajamas clearly worn. Dianne got the candlesticks. Tim got the two lilac bushes, one French purple, the other white—an alarming gift, lilacs being so evocative of the depth and dumbness of death's kingdom that they made Tim cry. They were large and had to be removed with a backhoe, which did not please the landlord, who didn't get anything, although he didn't have to return the last month's deposit either. Lucretia got the Manhattan glasses. They were delicate, with a scroll of flowers etched just beneath the rim. There were four of them. Andrew got the wristwatch. Betsy got the barbells. Jack got a fairly useless silver bowl. Angus got the photo basket whose contents he kindly shared. Louise got the dog.

Louise would have preferred anything to the dog, right down to the barbells. Nothing would have pleased her even more. It was believed that the animal had been witness to the suicide. The dog had either seen the enactment or come into the room shortly afterwards. He might have been in the kitchen eating his chow or he might have been sitting on the porch, taking in the entire performance. He was a quiet, medium-size dog. He wasn't one of those dogs who would have run for help. He wasn't one of those dogs who would have attempted to prevent the removal of the body from the house.

Louise took the dog immediately to a kennel and boarded it. She couldn't imagine why she, of all people, had been given the dog. But in the note Elliot had left he had clearly stated, *And to Louise my dog, Broom.* The worst of it was that none of them remembered Elliot's having a dog. They had never seen it before, but now suddenly there was a dog in the picture.

"He said he was thinking of getting a dog sometime," Jack said.

"But wouldn't he have said 'I got a dog'? He never said that," Dianne said.

"He must have just gotten it. Maybe he got it the day before. Or even that morning, maybe," Angus said.

This alarmed Louise.

"I'm sure he never thought you'd keep it," Lucretia said.

This alarmed her even more.

"Oh, I don't know!" Lucretia said. "I just wanted to make you feel better."

Louise was racking up expenses at the kennel. The dog weighed under thirty-five pounds but that still meant eleven dollars a day. If he had weighed between fifty and a hundred, it would have been fourteen dollars, and after that it went up again. Louise didn't have all that much money. She worked at a florist's and sometimes at an auto-glass tinting establishment, cutting and ironing on the darkest film allowable by law, which at twenty percent was less than most people wanted but all they were going to get. Her own car had confetti glitter on the rear window. It was like fireworks going off in the darkness of her glass.

She was sitting alone in a bar one evening after work worrying about the money it was costing to board the dog, who had been at the kennel for a week and a half. Louise had her friends, of course, and she saw them practically constantly, but sometimes she liked to be alone. Occasionally, she even took trips by herself, accompanied only by strangers, cruises or camping trips to difficult places where she was invariably lonely and misunderstood. These trips reminded her of last evenings, one of those last evenings which occur over and over in one's life, and she thought of them as good training. She had learned a lot from them. More than enough by now, probably.

In the bar was a long fish tank which served as a wall separating the restaurant beyond. Louise had never been in this place before and would not select it again. She didn't like to look at the fish, one of which was trailing a cloud of mucus behind it. In the restaurant beyond the fish she saw an older man deep in conversation with a party or parties outside her vision. He had moist, closely cut hair and a Band-Aid high up on his temple. A line of blood extended several inches down from the Band-Aid. Louise became engrossed in watching him chatting and smiling and sawing away at his steak or whatever it was. But she looked away for a moment and when she looked back the blood was gone. He must have wiped it away with a napkin, perhaps dipped in his water glass. Someone in the party he was with was fond of him or even possibly more than fond and told him about the blood. That was Louise's first thought, though it had certainly taken them long enough to mention it.

The next morning she went to the kennel. A girl brought the dog out. It had yellowish wavy fur.

"Is that the right one?" Louise asked. The girl looked at her expressionlessly and cracked her gum. "It's really not mine," Louise explained, "it belongs to a friend."

The dog crouched miserably on the floor in the backseat of Louise's car. It didn't even lie down.

"You're going to get sick down there," Louise said. The dog was clearly not habituated to riding in cars, and had no sense of the happiness it could bring.

After a week, she had discerned no habits. The dog didn't seem morose, merely withdrawn. She began calling it Broom with a certain amount of reluctance.

Every other week, there would be a party at one of their houses, though it wasn't Louise's turn just yet. Rent was cheap, so they all lived in these big ruined houses. She went over to Jack's and everyone was already there, drinking gimlets and looking at a rat Jack had caught beneath the sink on one of his glue traps.

"I'm not going to use these things again," Jack said. "They're depressing."

"I use them," Walter said, "but I never get any rats."

"You're not putting them in the right places," Jack said.

The rat watched them in a sort of theatrical way.

One of the twins, Wilbur, got up and opened a window. He picked up the trap and sailed it with its rat accompanist into the street to fall amidst the passing traffic.

"I usually take it down to the Dumpster," Jack said.

Wilbur and his twin, Daisy, were the only ones who said they remembered Broom. They said that he hadn't eaten from a bowl but off a Columbia University dinner plate. But in their far-out nods Wilbur and Daisy could picture almost anything. They spent most of their time lovingly shooting each other up. They had not been acknowledged in the note as gift recipients, although of course they didn't care. They insisted that matters would not have taken such a dreary turn had they been able to introduce Elliot to the great Heroisch, the potent, powerful, large and appealing Heroisch. The twins were so innocent they got on everyone's nerves. They loved throwing up on junk. A joy develops, they'd say, a real joy. It's not like throwing up at all.

They all had their big, quietly rotting houses, even the twins. Louise had a solarium in hers that leaked badly. In the rear was an overgrown yard with a birdhouse nailed to each tree. Some trees had more than one. The previous tenant must have been demented, Louise thought. How could they imagine that birds want to live like that?

At Jack's they drank, but lightly except for Dianne, who was drinking far too much recently. She'd said, "I began to wonder if it was worthwhile to undertake what I was doing at the moment. Pick a moment, any moment. I began to wonder. If I only had today and not tomorrow, would it be worthwhile to undertake what I was doing at the moment? I addressed myself to that very worthwhile question and I had to admit, well, no."

But no one tried to interfere with Dianne. They were getting over the death of their friend Elliot—each in his or her own way was the understanding.

"It takes four full seasons to get over a death," Angus said. "Spring and summer, winter and fall."

"Fall and winter," Andrew said.

Everyone was annoyed with Angus because he had taken

all the photos out of the flat woven basket where they'd always been kept and arranged them in albums, ordered by years or occasions. This pleased no one. It wasn't the same. The effect was different. Everything had looked like a gala before. Now none of it did.

They talked about the things Elliot had given them. They could not understand what he had been attempting to say. All his other possessions had been trucked away and stored. A brother was supposed to come for them. He was sick or lived in Turkey or some goddamn place, who cared. In any case, he hadn't shown up here yet.

Louise didn't think it was right that she had been given something alive. The others hadn't been given anything alive. She made this point frequently but no one had an explanation for it.

The twins had been reading Pablo Neruda and had come across the line *Death also goes through the world dressed like a broom,* but they weren't going to tell Louise that. *Dressed* didn't seem right anyway, maybe it was the translation. But Neruda was a giant among pygmies, his mind impeccable. They were going to keep their mouths shut.

More than a month passed. Louise was working full time in the florist's shop. She liked working there, at the long cutting table, wearing an apricot-colored smock among the unnatural blooms. A woman came in one day just before closing. She wanted to send a dozen roses to a young veterinarian assistant.

"My dog bit her when she tried to lift him for an X-ray," the woman said. "I'm so embarrassed."

Louise had never been interested in the reasons people bought flowers. "I don't like dogs," Louise said.

"Really?" the woman said. "I don't know where I'd be without my Buckie."

"You wouldn't be in here buying these roses," Louise said.

Another season insinuated itself. It was Tim's turn to give a party but things were not going well for him. The lilacs had not survived transplanting. They would never come back. Tim had done his best, but his best wasn't good enough. He had also had an unhappy experience with a pair of swans. He had been following their fortunes ever since he had witnessed them mating in a marsh beside the highway. "They twined their necks like heraldry afterwards," he said. "Heraldry." But after weeks of guarding the nest the male disappeared, and a week later the female vanished. Tim had watched them so arduously and suddenly they were gone. He was sure someone had murdered them. "Remember the lied about the swan?" he asked.

"Leda and the swan?" Angus volunteered.

"The German song," Tim said impatiently. "The *lied*," he said, upset.

It was about a swan who so loved a hunter by the marsh that she became a woman and married him and had three children. Then one night the king of the swans called to her to come back or else he would die, so slowly she turned into a swan again, slowly opened her wide white wings and left her husband and her children . . .

"Her wide white wings," Tim said, weeping.

Lucretia gave a party out of turn. Everyone came except Dianne and Tim. Walter asked Louise about the dog.

"Old Broom," Louise answered. "Poor Broom." The dog was not demanding. It was modest in its requirements. It could square itself off like a package in a chair, it could actually resemble a package, but that was about it. Everyone half expected that Broom would have disappeared by now, run away. "Listen," Lucretia said. "I'll tell you. One of those glasses I was given got a little chip on the rim and I found myself going to a jeweler's and getting an estimate for filing it down. It cost seventy-five dollars and I paid for it, but I'm not picking it up. I didn't even give them the right telephone number. I decided, enough's enough."

Walter confessed that he had thrown away the silk pajamas immediately, without a modicum of ceremony.

"None of it makes a bit of sense," Betsy said. "What would I want with barbells? I took those barbells down to the park and left them by the softball field. You're a saint, Louise. I could see you maybe not wanting to take it to the pound, but I always thought, She's going to take it to a no-kill facility.

"What do you mean?" Louise asked.

"A no-kill facility. Isn't that self-explanatory?"

"Well, no," Louise said, "not really. I mean it doesn't sound all that great somehow."

"Most places keep unwanted pets for two weeks and then, if they're not adopted, they put them to sleep."

"Put them to sleep," Louise said. She didn't know anybody said that anymore and here was her friend, Betsy, saying it. It sounded like something you'd do with a small child in a pretty room while it was still light out.

"And these people never do. I've just heard about these places, I've never seen one. I don't think there are many of them, but they are around."

"I don't like the sound of it either," Andrew said, "oddly enough."

"You know that woman came into the florist's the other

day to buy roses and I said to her, 'Oh no! Has Buckie bitten someone again?' " Louise said.

Her friends looked at her.

"And she said, 'I don't know what you're talking about.' " Louise laughed. "She was pretending she wasn't the same person."

Louise always wanted to talk about Broom with the others until they actually wanted to discuss him, then she didn't want to anymore.

Early one evening after work, Louise was sitting on the front steps of her house when a van pulled up across the street and a man got out. Louise was startled to see him walk over to her. He was deeply tanned with a ragged haircut. The collar of his shirt was too big for him.

"How do you do, Louise?" he said. "I'm Elliot's brother."

Louise cast herself back, remembering Elliot. She found him with more difficulty than usual, but then she had him, Elliot, she could see him. It was still him, exactly. Powerful Elliot. She said to the man, "You don't look at all like Elliot."

He seemed to be waiting for her to say more. When she didn't, he said, "I've been ill and out of the country. I couldn't travel. Travel was impossible, but I got here as soon as I was able. Elliot and I had quarreled. You can't imagine the pettiness of our quarrel, it was over nothing. We hadn't spoken for two years. I will never forgive myself." He paused. "I heard that he had a dog and that you have it now and it might be something of a burden to you. I'd like to have the dog. I'd like to buy it."

"I couldn't do that," Louise said simply.

"I insist on paying you something."

"No, it's impossible. I won't give the dog up," Louise said. He could be a vivisector for all she knew.

"It would mean a great deal to me," he said, his mouth trembling. "My brother's dog."

Louise shook her head.

"I can't believe this," he muttered.

"Believe what?" Louise said, looking at Elliot's brother, if that's who he was, although there was no reason to doubt him, not really.

He spoke again, patiently, as if she had utterly misunderstood his situation and the seriousness of his request. His guilt was almost holy, he was on a holy quest. He had determined that this was what must be done, the only thing that remained possible now to do.

"We were so close," he said. "He was my little brother. I taught him how to ski, how to drive. We went to the same college. I'd always protected him, he looked up to me, then there was this stupid, senseless quarrel. Now he's gone forever and I'm all ruined inside, it's destroyed me." He rubbed his chest as if something within him really was harrowed. "If I could care now for something he had cared for, then I would have something of my brother, of my brother's love."

"I don't mean to sound rude," Louise said, "but we've all been dealing with this for some time now and you suddenly appear, having been ill and out of the country both at the same time. Both at the same time," she repeated, for it seemed, though not unlikely, inane. "It's just so unnecessary now, your appearance. It's possible to come around too late."

"That's not true," he said. He was sallow beneath his tan. "Your friends, Elliot's friends, said they were sure you'd appreciate the opportunity, that they were sure you wouldn't mind, that in fact you'd be relieved and delighted."

"That just shows how little we comprehend one another," Louise said. "Even when we try," she added. "Have you ever had a dog before?" Louise was just curious. She didn't mean to lead him on, but as soon as she said this, she feared she'd given him hope.

"Oh yes," he said eagerly. "As boys we always had dogs."

"They'd die and you'd get another?"

"That's a queer way of putting it."

"Look," Louise said, "your brother had this dog for about three minutes." She felt she was exonerating Elliot.

"Three minutes," he said, bewildered.

"I said about three minutes. You should get a dog and pretend it was your brother's and care for it tenderly and that will be that." Louise was not going to get up and go inside the house and lock the door against him. She would wait him out. "There's nothing more to discuss," she said.

He turned from her sadly. There were several youths peering into his van. "Get away from there!" he cried, and hurried toward them.

It was Walter's turn to give a party. He had a fire in the fireplace although it wasn't at all cold. Still, it was very pleasant, everyone said so.

"I ordered half a cord of wood but it wasn't split, it was just logs," Walter said, "and one of the logs had a chain partly embedded in it, like a dog chain. The tree had started to grow right over the chain."

"Wow," Daisy said. "I don't think so."

"Sometimes," Wilbur said, "certain concepts, it's better not to air them."

The twins held each other's hands and looked into the fire.

"Who would have thought that Elliot would have such a dreary brother," Angus said. "I wouldn't have given him the dog either."

"Still, I'm amazed you didn't, Louise," Jack said.

"I guess he got all the things we actually remembered Elliot having," Andrew said. "I remember a rather nice ship's clock, for instance. That wristwatch I was given, who'd ever seen that before?"

"Elliot wasn't in his right mind," Betsy said. "We keep forgetting that. He wasn't thinking clearly. If you're thinking clearly, you don't take your own life."

Again, Louise marveled at her friend's way of phrasing things. To take your own life was to take control of it, to take possession of it, to give it a shape by occupying it. But Elliot's life still had no shape, even though it had been completed.

"I want to confess something," Andrew said. "I tossed that watch." He had crammed it into an overflowing Goodwill bin in the parking lot of a shopping mall. He described the experience of pushing the watch into an open-throated, softly bulging sack as an extremely unpleasant one. Everyone knew the Goodwill bin and the mute congregation of displaced things attending it, too large to have been slipped inside, all those things waiting to be revisited in this life, waiting to be used again.

That evening everyone drank too much and later dreamed vivid dreams. The twins dreamed they were in the middle of a highway, trying to cross, trying to cross. Angus dreamed he was in a coffee shop where a kindly but inefficient waitress who looked like his mother was directing him to a table that wasn't there. Lucretia dreamed she was carving *Kindertotenlieder* as sung by Kathleen Ferrier out of a block of wood with a chain saw. That's quite good, someone was saying. It's only a copy, Lucretia demurred. Walter dreamed he was kneeling at the communion rail in the silk pajamas. The cup was working its way toward him but had become a thermometer to be placed beneath the tongues of the devout, and by the time it reached him it was a dipstick from a car's engine that a mechanic was wiping with a filthy cloth.

Louise had had the dog for five months now. When she realized how much time had passed, she thought: Seven more months to go. In seven months we'll know more.

Someone was putting a house up behind Louise's house. The yard had been bladed and most of the trees taken down. The banal framework of a house stood there. When Louise gave a party, everyone was shocked at the change.

"I thought that yard went with this house," Jack said.

"Well, I guess not," Louise said.

"All those little birdhouses are gone," Lucretia said. "People put them inside now, you know, as a decorative accent. They paint them in these already fading, flaking colors and put them around."

"They're safer inside," Angus said.

"That thing is going to be huge, Louise," Betsy said. "It's going to loom over you."

They talked for a while about what she could plant to block it out.

"Nothing will grow in time," Betsy said.

"In time for what?" Walter said.

"Everything takes so long to grow. My god, Louise," Betsy said, "you'd better just move."

"Louise," the twins said, "if you die are you going to leave us anything?" They were sitting on the sofa eating pretzels.

Outside, the wind was blowing hard but there were no trees anymore to indicate this with their tossing branches. A door blew open, banging, though.

Louise was going to move. She didn't want that house going up behind her. Within a week, she had found another place. Walter and Lucretia helped her move. Walter had a truck and they transferred all the furniture in one trip. They transferred Broom too, with his dog bed and his dish for water and his dish for food. Then Louise packed her car with what remained, right up to the roof. Even so, she had thrown away a lot of things. She was simplifying and purifying her life, keeping only her nicest, most singular things. Louise swept the old house clean, glad to be leaving. She looked with satisfaction at the empty rooms, the stark windows and their newly ugly vistas. She slammed the door and headed for her car but it wasn't where she'd left it. She stared at the place where the car had been. But it had vanished, been stolen, and everything was gone. The sun was bright, still shining on the place where it had been.

It was Betsy's turn to have a party. They told theft stories—they all had them—and tried to cheer Louise up. She had already bought another car with the insurance money. It wasn't as appealing but she liked it in a different way. She liked it because she didn't like it that much, wasn't as girlishly pleased with it as she had been with the other one.

"You can get all new clothes," Lucretia said. "You can go on a spree. That favorite dress of yours had a spot on it anyway and kind of on the back at that."

"It did not," Louise said. "I got that spot out. I loved that dress."

"I bet you can't even remember everything you packed in the car," Jack said.

"My pearls," Louise said sadly.

"Christmas is coming," Angus said. But he always said that, as if he were going to buy everyone wonderful gifts, the gifts of their most perfect desiring. But he bought champagne and cookies that they would drink and eat was all.

"My grandmother's silver tea service."

"Louise, you know you never used that and would never use that in your life," Lucretia said. "It didn't have a place."

"But it's gone," Louise said. It was gone, of course, but there was something else, something worse. She had made all these choices. She had discarded this and retained that and it hadn't mattered.

"Things are ephemeral," Daisy said.

"And an illusion," Wilbur said.

"Well, which is it?" Jack demanded, annoyed.

Everyone was a little embarrassed. Seldom did anyone respond to the twins.

"I'll tell you one thing," Jack said, "I sold that crazy bowl of Elliot's to an antique store."

None of them could think about Elliot without being thwarted by the mystery of the things he'd given them. His behavior had been inexplicable. It was all inexplicable.

"Oh, I can't think about it anymore!" Louise cried. They were all drinking margaritas out of silly glasses.

"How is Broom?" Andrew asked delicately.

"Oh, I've rather gotten used to Broom," Louise said.

Lucretia looked at her unhappily. Louise had lost her sparkle, Lucretia thought.

Louise settled quickly into her new house. It was bigger than the other one and more ordinary. Broom didn't know which room to disappear into. He had tried them all and couldn't decide. He would take up in the most unlikely places. Sometimes she would come across him on the fifth step of a narrow back staircase. What an odd place to be! Wherever he was he looked uncomfortable. Still, she was sure Elliot would not have wanted her to surrender the animal so easily. Of course she would never know Elliot's thoughts. She herself could only think—and she was sure she was like many others in this regard, it was her connection with others, really—that life would have been far different under other circumstances, and yet here it wasn't, after all.

ANODYNE

MY MOTHER BEGAN going to gun classes in February. She quit the yoga. As I understand it, yoga is concentration. You choose an object of attention and you concentrate on it. It may be; but need not be, the deity. This is how it was explained to me. The deity is different now than it used to be, it can be anything, pretty much anything at all. But even so, my mother let the yoga go and went on to what was called a ".38"—a little black gun with a long barrel—at a pistol range in the city. Classes were Tuesday and Thursday evenings from five to seven. That was an hour and a half of class and half an hour of shooting time. I would go with her and afterwards we would go to the Arizona Inn and have tea and share a club sandwich. Then we would go home, which was just the way we left it. The dogs were there and the sugar machine was in the corner. We left it out because we had to use it twice a day. I knew how to read it and clean it. My mother and I both had diabetes and that is not something you can be cured of, not ever. In another corner was the Christmas tree. We liked to keep it up, although we had agreed not to replace any of the bulbs that burned out. At the same time we were not waiting until every bulb went dark before we took the tree down, either. We were going to be flexible about it, not superstitious. My grandmother had twelve orange-juice glasses. A gypsy told her fortune and said she'd live until the last of the twelve glasses broke. The gypsy had no way of knowing that my grandmother had twelve orange-juice glasses! When I knew my grandmother, she had seven left. She had four left when she died. The longest my mother and I ever left the tree up was Easter once when it came early.

This is Tucson, Arizona, a high desert valley. Around us are mountains, and one mountain is so high there is snow in the winter. People drive up and make snowmen and put them in the backs of their trucks and on the hoods of their cars and drive back down again, seeing how long they will last. My mother and I have done that, made a little snowman and put him on the hood of the car. There are animals up there that don't know that the animals below them in the desert even exist. They might as well be in different galaxies. The mountain is 9,157 feet tall, and is 6,768 feet above the city. Numbers interest me and have since the second grade. My father weighed one hundred pounds when he died. Each foot of a saguaro cactus weighs one hundred pounds, and that is mostly water. My father weighed no more than one cactus foot. I weigh sixty-eight pounds, my mother weighs one hundred and sixteen, the dogs weigh eighty each. I do my mother's checkbook. Each month, according to the bank, I am accurate to the penny.

The man who taught the class and owned the firing range was called the Marksman. He called his business an Institute. The Pistol Institute. There were five people attending the class in addition to my mother, three women and two men. They did not speak to one another or exchange names because no one wanted to make friends. My mother had had a friend in yoga class, Suzanne. She was disturbed that my mother had dropped the yoga and was going to the Institute, and she said she was going to throw the I Ching and find out what it was, exactly, my mother thought she was doing. If she did, we never heard the results.

My mother was not the kind of person who lived each day by objecting to it, day after day. She was not. And I do not mean to suggest that the sugar machine was as large as the Christmas tree. It's about the size of my father's wallet, which my mother now uses as her own.

When my father died, my mother felt that it was important that I not suffer a failure to recover from his death and she took me to a psychiatrist. I was supposed to have twenty-five minutes a week with the psychiatrist, but I was never in his office for more than twenty. Once he used some of that time to tell me he was dyslexic and that the beauty of words meant nothing to him, nothing, though he appreciated and even enjoyed their meanings. I told him one of our dogs is epileptic and I had read that in the first moments of an epileptic attack some people felt such happiness that they would be willing to give up their life to keep it, and he said he doubted that a dog would want to give up its life for happiness. I told him dead people are very disappointed when you visit them and they discover you're still flesh and blood, but that they're not angry, only sad. He dismissed this completely, without commenting on it or even making a note. I suppose he's used to people trying things out on him.

My mother did not confide in me but I felt that she was unhappy that February. We stopped the ritual of giving each other our needles in the morning before breakfast. I now gave myself my injections and she her own. I missed the other way, but she had changed the policy and that was that. She still kissed me good morning and good night and took the dogs for long walks in the desert and fed the wild birds. I told her I'd read that you shouldn't feed the birds in winter, that it fattened up the wrong kind of bird. The good birds left and came back, left and came back, but the bad ones stayed and were strengthened by the habits of people like my mother. I told her this to be unpleasant because I missed the needles together, but it didn't matter. She said she didn't care. She had changed her policy about the needles, not the birds.

The Pistol Institute was in a shopping mall where all the other buildings were empty and for lease. It had glass all across the front and you could see right into it, at the little round tables where people sat and watched the shooters and at the long display case where the guns were waiting for someone to know them, to want them. When you were inside you couldn't see out, because the glass was dark. It seemed to me the reverse of what it should be, but it was the Marksman's place so it was his decision. Off to the right as you entered was the classroom and over its door was the sign *Be Aware of Who Can Do Unto You.* No one asked what this meant, to my knowledge, and I would not ask. I did not ask questions. I had started off doing this deliberately sometime before but by now I did it naturally. Off to the left behind a wall of clear glass was the firing range.

The shooters wore ear protectors and stood at an angle in little compartments firing at targets on wires that could be brought up close or sent farther away by pressing a button. The target showed the torso of a man with large square shoulders and a large square head. In the left-hand corner of the target was a box in which the same figure was much reduced. This was the area you wanted to hit when you were good. It wasn't tedious to watch the shooters, but it wasn't that interesting either. I preferred to sit as close as possible to the closed door of the classroom and listen to the Marksman address the class.

The Marksman stressed awareness and responsibility. He stressed the importance of accuracy and power and speed and commitment and attitude. He said that having a gun was like having a pet or having a child. He said that there was nothing embarrassing about carrying a gun into public places. You can carry a weapon into any establishment except those that serve liquor, unless you're requested not to by the operator of that establishment. No one else can tell you, only the operator. Embarrassment is not carrying a gun, the Marksman said. Embarrassment is being a victim, naked, in a bloody lump, gazed upon by strangers. That's embarrassment, he said.

The Marksman told horrible stories about individuals and their unexpected fates. He told stories about doors that were opened a crack when they had been closed before. He told stories about tailgating vehicles. He told a story about the mini-van mugger, the man who hid under cars and slashed women's Achilles tendons so they couldn't run away. He said that the attitude you have toward others is important. Do not give them the benefit of the doubt. Give them the benefit of the doubt and you could already be dead or dying. The distinction between dead and dying was an awful one and I often went into the bathroom, the one marked *Does,* and washed my hands and dried them, holding and turning them for a long time under the hot-air dryer. The Marksman told the story about the barefoot, barechested madman with the machete on the steps of the capitol in Phoenix. This was his favorite story, illustrating as it did the difference between killing power and stopping power. The madman strode forward for sixteen seconds after he had been warned and his chest blown out. You could see daylight through his chest. You could see the gum wrappers on the marble steps behind him right through his chest. But for sixteen seconds he kept coming, wielding his machete, and in those sixteen seconds he annihilated four individuals. My mother kept taking the classes, so I heard this story more than once.

My mother decided that she wanted to know the Marksman socially and invited him to dinner along with the others in the class. We decided on a buffet-style arrangement, the plates and silverware stacked off to the side. This way, if no one came, we wouldn't feel humiliated. The table had not been set. No one came except the Marksman. Not the fat lady who had her own pistol and a purple holster for it, not the bald man or the two college girls, not the other man with the tattoo of a toucan on his arm. The Marksman was a thin man in tight clothes and he wore a gold chain and had a small mustache. Sometimes he favored bloused shirts but that night he was wearing a jacket. I sat with him in the living room while my mother was in the kitchen. The dogs came in and looked at him. Then they jumped up onto the sofa and curled up and looked at him.

"You allow those dogs every license, I see," he said.

I wanted to say something but had no idea what it was.

He asked me if I'd been to Disneyland.

"No," I said.

"How about the other one, the one in Florida?"

I said that I hadn't.

"Where are you from?" he asked me.

"Here," I said.

"I'm from San Antonio," he said. "Have you ever been to San Antonio?"

"No," I said.

"There's a big river there, a big attraction, that runs right past all the shops and restaurants and that's all lit up with fairy lights," the Marksman said. "Tourists take cruises on it and stroll beside it. They promenade," he said in a careful voice. "Once a year, they pump the whole thing out, the whole damn river, and clean it and then put the water back in again. They scrub the bottom like it was a bathtub and fill it up again. What do you think about that?"

My hands were damp. I was beginning to worry about this, but my mother always said there was nothing more useless than dreading something you weren't understanding.

"People have lost their interest in reality," the Marksman said.

· · ·

The classes continued at the Institute. The old group left and a new one with the same silent demeanor took their place. I stayed close to the door and listened. The Marksman said never to point the muzzle of a gun at something you weren't willing to destroy. He said that often with practice you're just repeating a mistake. He stressed caution and respect. He stressed response, readiness and alertness. When class was over, everyone filed out to choose a handgun and buy a box of ammunition, then strode to their appointed cubicle.

My mother did not extend any more dinner invitations to the group, although the Marksman came every Friday. It became the custom. I knew my mother did not exactly want him in our life, because she already was making fun of his manner of speaking, but she wanted him somehow. There are many people who have artificial friendships like this that become quite fulfilling, I'm sure. I tried to imagine him living with us. The used targets papering the rooms, his bloused shirts hanging on the clothesline, his enormous black truck in the driveway. I imagined him trying to turn my father's room into a saferoom, for the Marksman spoke often about the necessity of one of these in every house. The requirements were a solid-core door, a dead bolt, a wireless telephone and a gun, and this was the place you should immediately go to when a threat presented itself, a madman or a fiend or merely someone who, for whatever reason, wanted to kill you and cease your life forever. My father had died in his room, but the way I understood it, with very few modifications it could be made into a saferoom of the Marksman's specifications.

The psychiatrist had said that my father had been fortunate to have his room, in his own home with his own family, that is my mother and myself and the dogs. I did not disagree with this.

I liked the Marksman's truck. One Friday night when we were eating dinner I told him so.

"That's because you're an American girl," the Marksman said. "Something in the American spirit likes great size and a failure to be subtle. Nothing satisfies this better than a truck."

The Marksman usually ignored me, but would address me

if I spoke to him directly. With my mother he was courteous. I think he liked her. She did not like him, and I didn't know what she was doing. She had not become a very good shot, either.

My mother and father loved each other. He had been big and strong before he got sick. He had favorite things, favorite meals and movies and places. He even had a favorite towel. It was a towel I'd had with big old-fashioned trains on it. He said he liked it because whichever way he dried himself he felt he was getting somewhere, but when he got sick he couldn't wash himself or dry himself or feed himself either. When he was very sick my mother had to be careful when she washed him or his skin would come off on the cloth. He liked to talk, but then he became too weak to talk. My mother said my father's mind was strong and healthy, so we read to it and talked to it, even though I grew to hate the thought of it. This hidden mind in my father's body.

The Marksman had been coming over for several weeks when he appeared one evening with a cake in a box for dessert. I told him that we couldn't have dessert, that we had the sugar. It had never come up before.

"What do you do on your birthday without cake?" he said.

"I have cake on my birthday," I said.

He didn't ask me when my birthday was.

I wanted to show him how I used the sugar machine, but didn't want to tell him about it. I took the lancet, which was in a plastic cylinder and cocked with a spring, and touched it against my finger to get a drop of blood. I squeezed the single drop onto the very center of the paper tab and put it into the machine. My mother was outside, in the back of the house, putting out fruit for the birds, halves of oranges and apples. I looked at the screen of the machine, acting more interested than I actually was, as it counted down and then made the readout. A hundred and twenty-four, it said.

"I'm all right," I said.

"You're an American girl," the Marksman said, watching me.

"What are you doing?" my mother said. We used the machine in the morning and the afternoon. We didn't use it at night.

"I'm all right," I said. "Nothing."

I took the pitcher of water off the dining table and busied myself by pouring some into the saucer of the Christmas tree stand. The tree wasn't taking water anymore. The room was sucking up the water, not the tree. But it looked all right. It was still green.

"Do you want to learn to shoot?" the Marksman asked me.

"Goodness no," my mother said. "Isn't there a law against that or something? She's just a child."

"No law," the Marksman said. "The law allows you certain rights—you, me, her, everybody."

I wondered if he was going to say I could be a natural, but he didn't.

"No," my mother said. "Absolutely not."

I didn't say anything. I knew I would not always be with my mother.

I went to the psychiatrist longer than my mother and I went to the Institute. We stopped going to the Institute and the Marksman stopped coming over for dinner. The last time I went to the psychiatrist there was a new girl in the waiting room. There had always been a little girl about my age and now there was this new one, an older one. We were all girls there. It was a coincidence, is my understanding, that there were no boys. The littlest one was cute. She had a pretty heart-shaped mouth and she carried a toy, a pink and purple dinosaur that she was always trying to give away. You could tell she liked it, that she'd had it probably since she was born, it was all worn smooth and gnawed in spots. Once I got there and she had another toy, a rabbit wearing an apron, and I thought that someone had actually been awful enough to take the dinosaur when she offered it. But it showed up with her again and she was back to trying to give it not just to me but to anyone who came into the waiting room. That seemed to be the little girl's problem, or at least one of them.

The new girl told us that she was there because her hair was thinning and making her ugly. It looked all right to me, but she said that it was thinning and that she had to spend an hour each day lying upside down with her head on the floor to stimulate its growth. She said that she had to keep the hairs in the sink after she washed it and the hairs in the brush and the hairs on her pillows. She said that she'd left some uncollected hairs on a blouse that her mother had put in the laundry, and that when she found out about it she'd become so upset that she did something she couldn't even talk about. The other girl, the one my age, said that our aim should be to get psycho-pharmacological treatment instead of psychotherapy, because otherwise it was a waste of time, but that's what she always said.

I was the last of us to see the psychiatrist that afternoon. When my time was almost up he said, "You're a smart girl, so tell me, what's your preference, the manifest world or the unmanifest one?"

95

It was like he was asking me which flavor of ice cream I liked. I thought for a moment, then went to the dictionary he kept on a stand and looked the word up.

"The manifest one," I said, and there was not much he could do about that.

THE OTHER WEEK

"THE FIRE DEPARTMENT charged us three hundred and seventy-five dollars to relocate that snake," Francine said.

"Must have missed that one," Freddie said. "Fire department was here? Big red truck and everything?"

"There was a rattlesnake on the patio and I called the fire department and they had a long . . . it was some sort of device on a pole, and they got the snake in a box and released it somewhere and it shouldn't have cost anything because that's one of the services they provide to their subscribers, which is why everyone knows to call the fire department when a snake shows up on one's patio. But we are not one of their subscribers, Freddie. I was informed of this after the fact. We have not paid their bill and their service is not included in our property taxes, which we likewise have not paid."

"Must've been taking a bathe."

"The charge is excessive, don't you think? They were here for five minutes."

"Why didn't you just smack the thing with a hoe?"

"It's very civilized of the fire department to effect live removal. Why aren't we one of their subscribers, Freddie? If the house started to burn down, they'd respond but it would cost us twenty-five thousand dollars an hour. That's what they told me when I called to complain."

"House isn't going to burn down."

"Freddie, why aren't you paying our bills?"

"No money," he said.

It was October in the desert and quite still, so still that Francine could hear their aged sheltie drinking from the bidet in the pool house. He was forbidden to do this. Francine narrowed her eyes and smiled at her husband. "What happened to our money?"

"It goes, Francine. Money goes. I haven't worked in almost three years. Surely you've noticed."

"I have, yes."

"No money coming in, and you were sick for a year. That took its toll."

"They never figured out what that was all about," Francine admitted.

"No insurance. Seventeen doctors. You slept eighteen hours a day. All you ate was blueberries and wheatgrass."

"Well, that couldn't have cost much."

"Like a goddamn mud hen."

"Freddie!"

"Seventeen doctors. No insurance. Car costs alone shunting you around to doctors cost more than four thousand that year, not including regular maintenance, filters, shocks and the like. Should've rotated the tires but I was trying to keep costs down."

"There was something wrong with my blood or something," Francine protested.

"Bought you a goddamned armload of coral bracelets. Supposed to be good for melancholia. Never wore them. Never gave them a chance."

"They pinched," Francine said.

"Even stole aspirin for you. Stole aspirin every chance I got."

"That was very resourceful."

"Oh, be sarcastic, see where that gets you. There's no point in discussing it further. We're broke."

The sheltie limped out into the sun, sated. He barked hoarsely, then stopped. He was becoming more and more uncertain as to his duties.

Francine went to the kitchen for a glass of water. She searched the refrigerator until she found a lemon, a small shriveled one from which she had some difficulty coaxing a bit of zestful juice. The refrigerator was full of meat. Freddie did the shopping and had overfamiliarized himself with the meat department.

"Broke," Francine said. He couldn't be serious. They had a house, two cars. They had a *gardener.* She returned to the living room and sat down opposite her husband. He was wearing a white formal shirt, stained, with the linkless cuffs rolled up, black shorts and large black sunglasses. His gaze was directed toward an empty hummingbird feeder.

"It's bats that drain that thing at night," Freddie said. "You don't have hummingbirds at all, Francine. You've got lesser long-nosed bats. They arrive in groups of six. One feeds while the others circle in an orderly fashion awaiting their turn. I enjoyed watching them of an evening. Can't even afford sugar water for the poor bastards anymore."

"What do you propose to do about our finances, Freddie?"

"Ride it out. Let the days roll on. You had your year of sleeping eighteen hours a day."

"But that was a long time ago!" Once she had been the type of person who didn't take much between drinks, as they say, but the marathon sleeping—it actually had been closer to twenty hours a day, Freddie always was a poor judge of time— had knocked the commitment to the sauce right out of her.

"Seventeen doctors. No insurance. Never found out what it was."

"I pictured myself then very much like a particular doll I had as a little girl," Francine mused. "She was a doll with a soft cloth body and a hard plastic head. She had blue eyes and painted curls, not real curls. The best part was that she had eyelids with black lashes of probably horsehair, and when you laid the doll on its back those hard little eyelids would roll down and dolly would be asleep. Have I ever told you that's how I pictured myself?"

"Many, many times," Freddie said.

Dusk arrived. A dead-bolt gold. Francine maintained an offended silence as vermilion clouds streamed westward and vanished, never again to be seen by human eyes. Freddie made drinks for them both. Then he made dinner, which they took separately. A bit less meat humming in the refrigerator now. Francine retired to the bedroom and turned on the television. The sheltie staggered in and circled his little rug for long minutes before collapsing on it with a burp. He smelled a little, poor dear.

. . .

Freddie in seersucker pajamas lay down beside her in the bed. He settled himself, then placed his hand in the vicinity of her thigh. A light blanket and a sheet separated his hand from the thigh itself. He raised his hand and slipped it beneath the blanket. But there was still the sheet. He worked his hand under the fabric until he finally got to her skin, which he patted.

They were watching a film which was vicious and self-satisfied, tedious and predictable, when in a scene that did not serve particularly to further the plot a dead actor was introduced to digitally interact with a living one.

The dead actor was acting away. "Look at that!" Francine said.

The scene didn't last long, it was just some cleverness. The dead actor seemed awkward but professional. Still this wasn't the scene he had contracted for. Watching, Francine knew a lot more than he did about his situation, but under the circumstances he was connecting pretty well with others.

"What are you getting so upset about?" Freddie said.

"Space and time," she said. "Those used to be the requirements. Space and time or you couldn't get into the nightclub. Our senses establish the conditions for the world we see. Kant said our senses were like the nightclub doorkeeper who only let people in who were sensibly dressed, and the criteria for being properly dressed or respectably dressed, whatever, was that things had to be covered up in space and time."

"Who said this?"

"Kant."

Freddie removed his hand from her thigh. "Something's been lost in your translation of that one, Francine. Why does one want to get into the nightclub anyway? Or that nightclub rather than another one?"

"We're the nightclub!" she said. "We're each our own nightclub! And the nightclub might want other patrons. Other patrons might be absolutely necessary for the nightclub to succeed!"

"I think it's a little late for us to be discussing Kant with such earnestness," Freddie said.

"You mean a little this night late or a little life late?"

He nodded, meaning both.

She snatched the blanket off the bed and walked through the darkened house to the patio. It was long past the hour when people in the neighborhood used the outside. It was a big concern among Francine's acquaintances, who were always vowing to utilize the outside more, but after a certain hour they stopped worrying about it. To many of Francine's acquaintances, the outside was the only flagellator their consciences would ever know.

She wrapped herself in the blanket and lay on the chaise longue. She was very uncomfortable. When she lay on it in the daytime she was not at all uncomfortable. Finally she managed to wander into sleep, a condition for which she was losing her knack. When she woke it was glaring day and the gardener's face was hanging over hers. His name was Dennis, Dennis the gardener who had been in their employ for years. She had never been stared at so thoroughly. She frowned and he drew back and stood behind her. He placed his fingers lightly on her forehead and ran them down her neck, then dragged them up again and rubbed her temples. The day was all around her. The refulgent day, she thought. His hand floated to just above her collarbone and she felt an excruciating pain as his thumb dug into the tendon there and scoured it. She screamed and struggled upright.

"That shouldn't hurt," he said mildly. "It's because you're so tense."

She hurried into the house and quickly dressed. There was no coffee. She required coffee, and there was none. The house was silent. Both Freddie and the sheltie were gone. He sometimes took the dog for a walk, which Francine had thought was kind before she learned that their destination was usually a small park on a dry riverbed frequented by emaciated and tactically brilliant coyotes. There had been several instances when a coyote had materialized and carried off some pet absorbed in peeing, frolicking or quarreling with its own kind and thus inattentive to personal safety. Francine had accused Freddie of being irresponsible, but he insisted that attacks were rare. More important was the *possibility* of attack, which gave distinction to an otherwise vapid suburban experience and provided a coherence and camaraderie among a group of people who socially, politically and economically had little in common. They were a fine bunch of people, Freddie assured her, and they shared a considerable pool of knowledge regarding various canine personality problems—fear biting, abandonment issues and hallucinations among them—as well as such physical disorders as mange, anal impaction, seizures and incontinence, to name only a few.

Francine searched hopelessly for coffee. Outside, Dennis had scooped up a large snake between the tines of a rake and was dropping it over the wall that separated their lot from the Benchleys'. It looked quite like the snake the fire department had recently removed. Dennis was being helpful but she would have to dismiss him. He would simply have to retreat to his life's ambition, which he had once told her was to run a security cactus ranch. There he would cultivate hybrids specific to sites, creating fast-growing, murderously flowering walls with giant devil's-claw spines that could scoop an intruder's throat out in a heartbeat.

She went outside. "Dennis," she began.

He turned toward her, not a young man. He had deep lines in his narrow face, running from his eyes to the corners of his mouth. They were not unattractive. If a woman dared to have lines like that she would naturally be considered freakish.

"Rattlesnakes don't have anyplace to go anymore," Dennis said.

The snake, deposited in a flower bed maintained by the Benchleys at a cost of great aggravation, set off in the direction of a large rock Francine knew to be fraudulent. It weighed little more than an egg carton and concealed a spare house key for the maid.

"Dennis, I'm afraid we must terminate your services. We haven't the money to pay you."

Dennis shrugged. "Nobody's paid me for coming on a year."

"Freddie hasn't been paying you?"

"Told me six months ago you didn't have any money. I come here because you remind me of Darla. When I first saw you I said to myself, Why, she's the spit and image of Darla, taking the years into account."

"'Spitting image,'" Francine said. "What on earth does that mean?"

"I'll talk any way you want to talk. You want me to talk less formal? I'm just so happy we're talking at last, like the more than friends we were meant to be."

"This is of no interest to me, but who is Darla?"

"Darla was my nanny when I was eight years old. She was ten years older than me."

Francine was shocked. A nanny! Though she did not want to believe herself a snob.

"Darla liked snakes."

"I don't *like*—"

"She had lots of stories about snakes. She told me, for instance, that the Mayans practiced frontal deplanation in newborn children so their heads would look like a rattlesnake's head. They bound up the newborn's soft little skull with weights. They believed snakes were sacred and that people with rattlesnake skulls would be more intelligent and creative. This had a positive, motivating psychological force on them. They became freer, more aware, bright and unusual. And I remember saying to Darla when she told me this that I wish someone had had the imagination and foresight to do that to me when I was first born because I wouldn't mind having a deeply ridged, crenellated head. And Darla said it was too bad but knowing my parents, which of course she did very well, it would never have happened were they given the opportunity for a thousand years, they still wouldn't have done it. They were very conservative. Not like Darla. Darla could leap up as high as her own shoulders from a standing position. Darla rocked! We lived in St. Louis, and once a year Darla and I would come out here to the desert, each spring for three years, and spend a week at a dude ranch and shoot bottles and ride mules and sleep in bunk beds. The corral is where Galore is now."

"Is that a new town?"

"Barbeques Galore is there."

"Oh," Francine said. She found this quite funny but decided to say in her most gracious manner, "Change can be quite overwhelming at times."

"That's right, that's right," Dennis said. "And then we'd come back to St. Louis and Darla would go off on another week of vacation but without me, and as you might imagine I resented that other week very much because I loved Darla. And then Darla had to have an operation."

"Wait," Francine said. "An operation?"

Dennis nodded. "She had to go under the anesthesia. And when a person goes under the anesthesia they're never the same when they come back up. You've got another person you're dealing with then. It makes just the smallest difference, but it's permanent. The change only happens once. That is, you might have to go under the anesthesia again for one reason or another and there'd be no change. Change don't build on that first change."

Why did she have to have an operation? Francine wondered.

"I was never told why she had to have an operation," Dennis said, "so that's not important."

She shouldn't have been jumping as high as her own shoulders, perhaps, Francine thought.

"We still talked about snakes and made pineapple upside-down cake and swam and rode bicycles and I was still in love with her and then she took her other week again, which I begrudged her as usual, and when she came back she died."

"I'll be darned!" Francine exclaimed. She really was trying to follow this unformed history. It would cost her nothing to be polite. They owed him money and he had done a good job with the citrus. Not a remarkable job, but a good one. Also, he was a human being who had suffered a loss, even if that loss had been by her estimation almost thirty years ago. The shock had clearly addled him. It must have come exactly at the wrong time. A moment either side of it and he would have been perfectly all right. She hoped they hadn't had an open casket.

"My parents permitted me to put a piece of broken glass in the coffin because Darla and I collected pieces of broken glass. It was one of the many collections we maintained. My parents didn't want there to be any confusion in my mind. They wanted me to realize that this time Darla was gone for good. Still, I had difficulty with the concept. It was a little beyond me."

"An open casket can sometimes backfire," Francine said.

"What?"

Darla sounded like a good-hearted girl, energetic, inventive, a nice kid, called too soon from life's parade or banquet, whatever it was. She couldn't imagine anyone being further from the idea of Darla than herself.

"I don't know what I would have done if I hadn't found you," Dennis said

"You haven't found me!" Francine said, alarmed.

"I'm not saying you *are* Darla, jeesh, I'm not crazy. I'm just wondering if you wouldn't like to go out some night and talk like we used to."

"I was never Darla."

"Jeesh," Dennis said. "I'm not saying you were Darla and now you're just not, I'm not crazy. But I was thinking we'd go out in the desert and build a little fire. Darla loved those fires so! I could bring the wood we'd need to get it started in the motorcycle's saddlebags. In less than fifty miles we could be in the desert. Fat Boy could get us there in an hour."

"We are in the desert."

"You know they don't know what this is now where we are."

He was missing a tooth, far back, it was way back, only noticeable in the way that hardly noticeable things are.

"You've seen my Harley. Haven't you just wanted to climb on Fat Boy and *go*? That bike gets so many compliments. If I ever wanted to sell, the ad would read *consistent compliments*, but I'll never sell. Or maybe you'd want to go somewhere else. I'll take you anywhere you want. I got another pair of jeans, newer jeans. What? My hearing's not so good. After Darla died I stuck knives in my ears. You know how they say you shouldn't put anything smaller than your elbow in your ear? It was in honor of Darla because I loved her voice so and never wanted to hear another's. I probably hear better than I should but I miss some of the mumble. You were mumbling there, not making yourself clear."

"The only place I'm going now, Dennis, is inside my home. I don't feel well."

"You don't look as good as you do sometimes. You got a headache? Darla used to have the cruelest headaches. I'd soak cloths in cool vinegar and put them on her head."

She probably had tumors the size of goose eggs in that head, Francine thought. Any operation was bound to be futile.

"OK, you go on inside," Dennis said. "Close the blinds. Put on this music I'm going to give you. Put this in your tape player. Take whatever's in there and throw it away. You'll never care for it again." He unbuttoned the pocket of his denim shirt and removed a plastic Baggie containing a tape. "It's Darla playing the piano. It was in the lodge at the dude ranch right where Galore is, as I've told you. We didn't have a piano in St. Louis. This is pure Darla. She was so talented! When you hear this you'll recognize everything for the first time."

"Music can't do that."

"It can't?" He pressed the tape into her hand. "Since when?"

. . .

There was still no coffee. She wasn't going to waste her time looking for coffee when there wasn't any. A moth was floating in the sheltie's water bowl. This was one of those recurrent things. She went into the bedroom and lay on the unmade bed. She wanted to sleep. She could no longer fall asleep! Insomnia, of course, was far worse than just being awake. She thought longingly of those two stages—the hypnagogic and the hypnapompic, although she could never declare with confidence which was which once she'd been informed of their existence—on either side of sleep, the going into and the coming out when the conscious and the subconscious were shifting dominance, when for an instant the minds were in perfect balance, neither holding dominion. But she couldn't sleep, she lacked her escorts, the hypnapompic and the hypnagogic— who had of late been acting more like unfriendly guards.

The sun was slipping into the afternoon, exposing the dirtiness of the windows, which she never cleaned in the hope of dissuading doves from crashing into the glass. The doves flew undissuaded. The many blurred impressions of their dove bodies depressed her but she was convinced that sparkling windows would be even more inviting to them as they attempted to thread their way among the houses in their evening plunge from the foothills to the valley below.

She had removed the tape from the dusty little bag and played it. It was a formal exercise—familiar, pleasant, ordinary playing. It didn't cast a spell or create a mood. It was not the kind of music that tore hungrily at her. It did not appeal to her at all. Much of the tape was empty of all but hum and hiss. The playing had simply stopped and had not resumed again. There was no applause, no exclamations of approval, no sense of an audience being present, least of all an impressionable child. Darla had certainly taken that kid for a ride. Had she confounded everyone she met in her brief life or only him? Probably him alone. She didn't think Dennis even knew this Darla very well, not really. He had a collection of queer memories—a girl leaping in place to what avail—of no more value than bits of broken glass. He had nothing. Darla inhabited his world more than he did, for she infused it, doing what the dead would like to do but in most cases couldn't, which in Francine's opinion was a very good thing. As far as she was concerned, though, Darla, her quenched double, was a disappointment.

She played the tape again and it sounded even less interesting than before and briefer as well. She didn't know what was missing, it had just become, was becoming, more compressed. She began to play it once more, then thought better of it. She ejected it from the machine and put it back in the Baggie. Locating a pencil, she tore an envelope in half—another unpaid bill!—and wrote:

*Dear Dennis. We appreciate the work
you've done. Good luck in raising
security cactus! Good-bye and all best.*

Her sentiments were not at all sincere but such were the means by which one expressed participation in the world.

Dennis was scrubbing the swimming pool tiles with a pumice stone.

"Here's your tape back," Francine said.

"It's something, isn't it," Dennis said.

"I found it a little repetitive."

"Yes, yes, those final chords can never be forgotten quickly enough." He seemed pleased.

"Dennis, I'm curious about a number of things."

"Darla was curious."

"You are from St. Louis and Darla is buried there?"

He nodded. "My family once owned half of St. Louis but they don't anymore."

"It seems a lot to be responsible for," she agreed. "But my point is, with you treasuring the memory of Darla so, I would think you would find her more present back there."

Dennis opened his mouth in a wide grimace. "Sorry," he said. "Darla always told me I eat too fast. Sometimes I can't catch my breath. I just had lunch."

"You could visit her grave and such," Francine went on relentlessly.

"That would be unhealthy, wouldn't it?" Dennis said. "Besides, Darla never liked St. Louis. She didn't care for vernacular landscapes. You couldn't see the stars in St. Louis. Darla liked a pretty night. No one liked a pretty night more than that girl did."

"She sounds like an exceptional young woman," Francine said dryly.

"She was beautiful and smart and kind and generous."

"I don't see her, Dennis. I can't picture her at all."

"And when she looked at you, she did it with her whole heart. You existed when she looked at you. You were . . ." He appeared to be short of breath again.

"I'm not a particularly nice person, Dennis. I've had to admit that to myself, and I'll admit it to you as well. I might have been nice once but I get by the best I can now. I don't even know how you'd look at someone, anything, with your whole heart. Why, you'd wear yourself out. You'd become nothing but a cinder. Life would become intolerable in no time. Now, it sounds as though you had a very fortunate childhood until you didn't. It's what I always think when I see cows grazing in the fields or standing in those pleasant little streams that wind through the fields or finding shade beneath the occasional tree, that they have a very nice life until they don't. An extreme analogy, perhaps—well, yes, forget that analogy, but you have to move on, Dennis. Your life's not assimilating your days and that's not good, Dennis."

"What?" Dennis said.

"Now I want you to read the note I've given you. And I really must find Freddie. He and the sheltie have been gone for an unusually long while."

Francine walked briskly through the patio to the garage. The door was open and Freddie's large dour Mercedes was gone, leaving only "her" car, an unreliable convertible she professed to adore. She would go to the dog park. She stepped into the convertible, turned on the ignition and studied the gauges. It was very low on fuel.

At the gas station, the attendant inside said, "What would you do if this wasn't a real hundred-dollar bill?"

"What would I do?"

"Yeah!" The girl had unnaturally black hair and a broad unwinning smile.

"Of course it's real. Do you think I'm trying to pass off a counterfeit?"

"Nah," the girl said, "I'm not going to take it. I'm using my discretion."

"It's a perfectly good bill," Francine said. "Don't you have a pen or a light or something that you pass over these things?"

"You have to give me something smaller. I'm using my discretion."

Francine was about to continue her protests but realized this would only prolong the girl's happiness. She returned to her car, annoyed but not so shaken that she failed to offer the moribund palm on the pump island her customary sympathy.

There was no dearth of gas stations. She broke the hundred and filled up the gluttonous little car. Then, after driving for miles and making several incorrect turns, she arrived at the dubious park. When she and Freddie had first moved to Arizona they had taken a rafting trip and everyone had gotten sick. The guide had not lost enthusiasm for his troubled industry, however. "Nobody likes to get sick from a little sewage!" he'd said. "But you're on the river! Some folks only dream of doing this!" This was another river, though, or had been.

A half dozen dogs rushed up to her. One had a faded pink ribbon attached somehow to the crown of its head, but none of them had collars. She tried to befriend them with what Freddie referred to as her birthday-party voice, though they seemed a wary lot and disinterested in false forms of etiquette.

She wondered which one of them had the hallucinations and what he thought was going on around him right then. She waded through the pack and approached a group of people sitting on a cluster of concrete picnic tables.

"Has a man with a sheltie been here today?"

"The sheltie," a woman said. "Congratulations!"

"I'm sorry?" Francine said.

"No need to be. It was a dignified departure, wasn't it, Bev?"

"As dignified as they come," Bev said. "We all almost missed it."

"I find it so much more convincing to see how things just happen rather than to observe how we, as human individuals, make them happen," a man said.

"Yeah, but we still almost missed it," Bev said, "even you." She winked at Francine. "He thinks too much," she confided.

"A swift closure," another man said. "One of the best we've seen."

Francine began to cry.

"What's this, what's this," someone said fretfully.

Francine returned to the car and drove aimlessly, crying, around the sprawling city. "Poor old dear," she cried. "Poor old dear." But I might have misunderstood those people completely, she thought. What had they said, anyway? She stopped crying. When it was almost dark she pulled up to a restaurant where she and Freddie had dined when they did such things. She went into the restroom and washed her face and hands. Then she opened her purse and studied it for a long moment before removing a hairbrush. She pulled the brush through her hair for a while and then replaced it. Slowly she closed the handbag, which as usual made a decisive click.

In the dining room, the maître d' greeted her. "Ahh," he said noncommittally. She was seated at a good table. When the waiter appeared she said, "I'm starving. Bring me anything, but I have no money. Tomorrow I can come back with the money." She was a different person. She felt like a different person saying this.

The waiter went away. Nothing happened. She watched the waiters and the maître d' observing her. On the wall beside her was a large framed photograph of a saguaro that had fallen on a Lincoln Brougham in the parking lot and smashed it good. Save for such references, one hardly knew one was in the desert anymore.

People came into the restaurant and were seated. They made their selections, were served and then left, all in an orderly fashion. A glass of water had been placed before Francine when she first sat down and she had drunk that and the glass had not been refilled.

She left before they flipped the chairs and brought out the vacuum cleaner. When she arrived home the garage door was still open and Freddie's Mercedes was not there. There would probably be a reminder in their mailbox the following morning that subdivision rules prohibited garage interiors to be unnecessarily exposed. No one likes to look at someone else's storage, they would be reminded. Francine very much did not want to go into the house and face once more, and alone, the humming refrigerator and the moth floating in the sheltie's water dish. Given Freddie's continued absence, she would probably have to call the police. But she did not want to call the police after her experience with the fire department. She considered both of these official agencies and their concept of correctness of little use to her. She eased the car into gear—it sounded as though something was wrong with the transmission again—and drove off once more into the dully glowing web of the city, lowering the roof and then raising it again, unable to decide if she was warm or cold. Finally she left the roof down, though no stars were visible. The lights of the city seemed to be extinguishing them by the week.

Stopped at a light at a large intersection, she saw the Barbeques Galore store. The vast parking area covered several acres and was dotted with dilapidated campers, for the store was not closed for the evening but had gone out of business, providing welcome good habitat for the aimless throngs coursing through the land.

She turned and, threading her way among the vehicles, heard the murmur of voices and saw the silhouettes of figures moving behind flimsily curtained windows. Some trucks had metal maps of the country affixed to the rear, the shapes of the states colored in where the people had been. Dangling from the windshield mirrors were amulets of all kinds, crosses, beads, chains. On the dashboards were cups, maps, coins and crumpled papers, even a tortoise nibbling on a piece of lettuce. And there, swooping in a grateful arc on the darkened margin of the place, Galore, the ineradicable locus of what had been his happiness, was Dennis on his waxed and violet Fat Boy. He hadn't seen her yet, of that she was sure. But if she went to him, what could be the harm? For he was no more than a child in his yearnings, and his Darla was just an exuberant young girl who could never dream she didn't have a life before her.

CLARO

Danny looked trim in shorts and a white T-shirt. He had been ill the previous year—the heart—but the operation was a success and he was now absolved of illness. It was remarkable, the skill of surgeons. Her sickness—her malady, she called it lightly—was of another sort, quite minor really. She had a form of arthritis, a syndrome called Polymyalgia rheumatica, and it was not known whether it was a disease of the joints, the muscles or the arteries. Statistically, she was rather young to be suffering from it. Though it wasn't particularly painful, she could barely move her limbs. Some of their friends had immigrated to Mérida for a good part of the year, and they too were now trying it out. The place was warm, cheap and genial, and the gardens could be lovely.

For breakfast there was sliced papaya, sweet rolls and good strong coffee. Their young man, their houseman Eduardo, was breakfasting comfortably with them, eating cereal, his favorite, Cap'n Crunch.

"Thank you," she said as Eduardo cleared away the plates.

She wanted to put more effort into the days, into the living of them. She was aware of the effort Danny was making. The days seemed very much the same here but this was just the seeming of them. Each delivered its own small surprise. Yesterday, sitting in the garden with only her aching body for company, she saw not just one but three motmots on the sloping tiled roof. They perched close together, their long, partially featherless tails flicking back and forth. The one in the center was being groomed by the other two. His feathers were ruffled and he looked dazed. Their heads were a lovely turquoise color. They preened and pecked at the one, drawing its feathers between their beaks. A frond from a royal palm slipped free and fell and two of the birds scattered at the sound, leaving the one upon whom their attention had been conferred alone, swaying, its beak open. Eduardo had hurried out and cut up the frond quickly with his knife. He hoisted the sections on his shoulder and trotted to the courtyard next door, the annex they had acquired to hold their construction and yard debris.

When he returned for the frond's heavy boot—almost as big as he was—Lilly called out, "Eduardo, you are not putting any pesticides in the garden, are you? Any poisons?"

"If it is not your wish, no."

"It certainly is not my wish."

"I do not," he said. He took off the floppy hat he wore and looked steadily at her.

The motmot then took flight, to her relief. It looked all right.

She liked Eduardo's little daughter, Stephanie, who was four. She was small and stout, not timid or incurious but solemn, with large dark eyes.

It was a new crowd here, though she could recognize them. There was the chatterer, the flatterer, the wag, the silent one. There was Stephen, who had found a new love. His other woman had been a horror, a terrible alcoholic, and that was a story. She'd passed out yet again and Stephen insisted that she see a doctor. With difficulty, he got her in the car. "You need help, Lucille," he shouted at her. He drove her to the doctor, the good one on Colón, but the office would not accept her because she was a corpse. He had to drive the body to the hospital himself. Neither would that institution receive her; no, she must be returned to where she died, their home, and only then could the authorities confirm her death and the proper procedures commence. Stephen was in traffic for an hour, making his ghastly circuit of the city, his dead wife beside him.

That, however, had been three years ago, and now another had found him, a good one, an American near his age with tremendous energy. They were restoring a hacienda on the road to Uxmal. Lilly and Danny had gone out there for lunch. The place was lovely but far from finished, of course. There was a chapel, and two of the stables were being turned into comfortable suites for tourists. They had ripped out all the henequen, which was not merely agave here, it was political. In the great courtyard a black garbage bag was caught in the topmost branches of a poinciana tree. Stephen's woman explained that it was not trash but a kite that one of the children had lost. They permitted the children to take a shortcut through the walled hacienda on their way to school. It was a kite. They were on good terms with the people of the village.

At lunch, one woman said, "I'm ordering a black lucite bed

with little lights embedded everywhere, and I'm seventy-two years old."

A man was talking about the coast. "In the morning, the ceviche is wonderful. Lunch, too, can be good. But dinner? Never. The sea's gifts begin to stink."

. . .

It was May 14, the day of St. Matthias, the thirteenth disciple, who was chosen by lot to replace the puzzle, Judas, that dark ordained deceiver. Matthias was a figure not of mystery but of disinterest. Nevertheless, he had his day.

Lilly was venturing out that morning to the English library, which was just around the corner, to take out storybooks for Stephanie. She wanted to teach the child how to read but had no idea of how to go about it. Stephanie was bright. Together they would find a way. They enjoyed each other's company immensely.

By the time Lilly reached the library, she was exhausted. She sank into a chair and the librarian was kind enough to offer her a glass of water. Her whole body ached. A small television set was on, tuned to an American news program. A man of much experience in strategic planning in both Republican and Democratic administrations, was discussing a matter of grave importance. He was calm, stunningly articulate, erudite. He slumped a little as he spoke. One could not argue with his analysis; no appeal was possible. He proceeded with the phrase *on the other hand*. Relentlessly, dispassionately, like a great weight falling. *On the other hand.* He reminded Lilly of the surgeon who had saved Danny, or rather repaired him. That had been a frightening time for them.

No, she reconsidered this. The surgeon had been worldly, certainly, but this man was of another cast. No dread was left unanticipated. Nothing had to be true. His thought was of a stunning circularity, seamless, unassailable. He was a man unconfused by the corrupting shapes of destiny.

"Feeling better?" the librarian asked.

"Oh . . . yes," Lilly said, startled. "I don't know what's wrong with me. Thank you for the water."

"Shall I turn this blowhard off?"

"I've had quite enough of it, thank you," Lilly said.

He was a lanky American with a thin, amused voice, rough skin and white, exceptionally white, teeth. His glasses were boyishly smudged. Betty Boop was tattooed on his forearm. "A symbol of my Jewish heritage," he said when he saw Lilly glancing at it. "Father's side." He put his hands on his hips.

"I'm looking for one or two simple storybooks," she said. "I'm trying to teach a little girl—a little friend of mine—the alphabet."

"I've just been organizing the children's section. Not my specialty. Half the books should be discarded, in my opinion. They look as though they've been eaten by goats." He frowned. "Someone gave us a whole set of Ant and Bee."

"I'm not familiar with that series," Lilly said.

"Twits from Great Britain. The rage for decades. I can't believe it's washed up here. An alphabetical story for tiny tots. Ant and Bee live in this goddamn cup and have a dog for a friend, get it?"

Lilly laughed.

"And the *dog* takes them for a ride on his back but they crush an *egg* on the road, not seeing it because of the *fog* which is so thick it causes him to trip over a *gun* and knock his *hat* off."

"A gun!" exclaimed Lilly.

"The illustrator's got the gun looking like a goddamn cannon, which is so confusing."

"I guess not Ant and Bee, then," Lilly said. "You're quite convincing."

"I was never the most reasonable child, but those two simply outraged my sense of the appropriate. My mother said again and again, 'Why are you fighting Ant and Bee?' Eventually she had to admit to the other mothers, 'Rockford simply hates Ant and Bee. Nothing can be done.'"

Lilly laughed.

"You're a good audience," he said, peering at her. He removed his smudged glasses and held them up to the light. "Wow," he said, "no wonder."

"There's some explanation as to why children's stories are so nonsensical," Lilly said, "but I can't remember it."

He was violently rubbing the glasses on the hem of his guayabera. "You're new here," he stated. "When people first come here they want to *do* something."

She walked stiffly to the shelf that held a ragged selection of picture books. "How many of these can I borrow?"

"Are you kidding! Take them all. No one's been in this place since the Second Annual Chili Cookout we had in the garden last week, a great turnout. People love their food booths. May I suggest what I believe? There was once a single language which all creatures possessed. It was highly complex and exceedingly beautiful. Latin was but a gross simplification of its glories. Then some sort of cataclysm, we can't even guess. Overnight, a soiled, simpler world of cruder possibilities. Words had to be invented, they became artificial. Over centuries we appeared to evolve but our language didn't. Words aren't much more than a waste product now, space junk. We're living post-literately. It's all gleanings and tailings. It's boring, it's transitory, but a counterliterate future is at hand. It's what's coming. The only thing language does now is separate us from the animals. We require something that separates us from ourselves."

"You're some librarian," Lilly ventured.

"I'm not the librarian. The librarian is imprisoned in the back. Furious, frightened. Gagged, bound."

"I'm smiling uncertainly now, I suppose," Lilly said.

"You're a nice lady," Rockford said. "Everyone will tell you I'm a foolish man. People can actually find me annoying." He raised his hands and pressed his fingers together. "Forgive me."

He took the books she had selected to a desk, put his glasses back on and wrote the titles down in a ledger. He consulted a calendar on the wall and recorded the date as well. Indeed it was St. Matthias's day, he for whom little had been imagined.

Walking home, she saw a thin donkey pulling a flat cart stacked with bags of cement. The reins were red.

. . .

"You know that prednisone is making your face puffy."

She didn't raise her hand to feel her bones. She would have once.

"Your lovely face," Danny continued. "A blurring."

"It's your glasses."

"What! I don't wear glasses."

"A joke," Lilly said.

"I wish I hadn't mentioned it."

"It's just a side effect. A known side effect. Nothing unusual."

"Of course. If it's helping you. That's the important thing."

"I don't know that it is. I've got to give it a chance to work, the doctor said."

"I'd read that the benefits were supposed to be more or less immediate."

She turned her head to the left, then to the right.

"See, you couldn't do that two weeks ago."

"I feel like a puppet," Lilly said.

"You'll be climbing the pyramids soon, singing at the top of your lungs. Then you'll run down, you'll *bound* down."

"I'm happy you feel so well, Danny."

"There's no obligation for you not to. It's not a trade-off." Though he sometimes entertained the disagreeable notion that it was.

· · ·

Eduardo looked at her with hostility, then his face broke into a warm smile.

"Why do you do that?" she asked. "Do you do it just for me?"

"*Qué?*"

She said nothing but watched as he raised his broad brown hand and slowly drew it across his face. There was the look of hostility and contempt once more.

"You are easy to tease," he said in a friendly manner.

· · ·

They had gone, as part of a small group, to visit the artist Iseabail. He lived in a slum, in a house he hadn't left for twenty years. The roof was falling in. The hurricane had destroyed the pond where he kept his pet carp. In the past, when it suited him, he had removed a carp for printmaking and feasts. The chandelier above the dusty table, still set formally for ten, was ribboned with strings of dirt. No more the notorious dinner parties, renowned for their delightfully surreal touches. Still, he painted every day. He favored working from photographs or postcards and was not averse to commissions. He was gracious, though the zipper on his pants was broken. All the Americans had a number of Iseabails. They were colorful and looked good on the high walls of their houses.

"Now you've met them both, Lilly," her friend Barbara said, "our pet zanies. But Rockford is just awfully fey, you know, whereas Iseabail is an artist and one not trying to formulate and impose some inner belief on anybody, thank god. I know you're going to say the eyes are off and it's true, he doesn't do the eyes as well as he should, but that's part of the charm. As for Rockford, the trick to dealing with him is just to say 'Really! Really, is that so!'"

. . .

Stephanie wore the same blue dress every time she visited. Lilly bought another dress which she kept folded in tissue in her closet. She planned to give it to the child when the moment seemed appropriate. This moment occurred when Stephanie, gripping a sandwich Lilly had prepared, squeezed a fat slice of tomato onto her lap. Lilly produced the new dress and convinced her that she should put it on while they washed the other one. Together they washed the blue dress in a pan of water—it seemed scarcely more than a rag—and hung it on the clothesline. Though the day was warm, there was no breeze and the fabric dried slowly. Stephanie examined it frequently to confirm that the awful stain was not reappearing. They did little more that day than watch the small dress dangling on the line. It was still damp when it was time for her to leave with her father and catch the bus that would take them home, thirty minutes away. Lilly wrapped it in a plastic bag. Eduardo did not remark on Stephanie's new dress or the parcel she held. He looked weary. His hair was white with plaster dust, as he had rewired an entire wall that day.

The next time Stephanie came to the house, she was wearing the same thin blue dress. Lilly never saw the other one again. The two of them did not discuss it.

· · ·

Rockford had been murdered, shot in his room in the library where he slept and took his meals. It was all anyone could talk about. There hadn't been a murder in decades. Nothing had been stolen, not even the rings on his fingers, and there were no suspects. Perhaps it was someone who resented the fact that the elderly woman whose modest *palacio* it had been willed the place for a library. There were certainly other things she could have done with the money. The rumor was that someone from Chiapas had done it. Everything unpleasant was blamed on someone from Chiapas.

· · ·

Lately she had been sleeping alone, in a room of her own just off the salon. It was the discomfort of her body, the constant tossing and turning. She was no one to share the night with, she'd be the first to admit. And since Rockford's death she'd been having nightmares. There would be a sense of tension in the air, then a figure separating from the shadows cast by the ungainly wardrobe. Something threatening was wielded—a gun?—a charge of extinguishing light was imminent, but there was still time, a skein of coiled time in which Lilly could act, could acknowledge and confront this thing which had come to take back something she didn't understand. Something had been given to her to understand and she simply wasn't strong enough to understand it. Still, she was strong enough to resist it being taken.

She would scream, whirl herself upright, fumble for the light, alarm the old dog, Amiga, the stray who sometimes slept beside her.

. . .

Danny had returned to Miami for a checkup with his doctor. He would be gone for five days. He would see the accountant and lawyer as well, for his father, it was suspected, was becoming senile.

Eduardo labored around the house, forever occupied. He didn't bring Stephanie with him, saying that she had an earache. Lilly was lonely. She had lunch with Barbara and Wilbur, after which they drove to Kabah and looked at the rain-god masks.

"Do you ever have difficulty with Arturo?" Lilly asked.

"No," Barbara said. "You don't like him? We're delighted

with him, we'd be lost without him. Wilbur just paid to have his teeth fixed. Four root canals! But he's a doll, just like your Eduardo."

Wilbur was trying to convince a carver in the souvenir palapa to come to their house and give him a price for carving one of the doors to the bathroom. It was a wonderful bathroom. "Can you reproduce one of Frederick Catherwood's scenes on a door?" Wilbur asked.

The man shrugged and said, "Sure," at the same time. He was carving a jaguar and smoothing the fresh cuts with a leaf. Two finished jaguars were available.

"Not that I expect it to be perfect," Wilbur said. "Just so people will recognize it as an illustration from Stevens's book." He said to Barbara, "I think this would be fun."

"When I first came here I thought all those jaguars on the facades were eating mangoes," Barbara confided to Lilly. "Finally someone told me, 'Barbara! That is a sacrificed human heart!'"

. . .

The day Danny was to return home, Eduardo came to her and said, "I must leave for at least a month. I must make money for a"—he paused—"unanticipated expense." He took off his hat and regarded it sullenly. "I must dig for a swimming pool for a whole month. It must all be done by hand, no dynamite."

"My husband will be disappointed," Lilly said. "Could you tell us what the problem is? Perhaps we could help."

"I cannot tell you."

She wanted to be more approving of Eduardo, who did a great deal for them. In general she did not like people much. It was said that there were certain trees that didn't like people. The ash? Perhaps she had once been such a tree, a solitary ash. The prednisone made for jumpy thoughts. The fact was, she failed to make connections with people. She liked children before they became closed and canny. She scratched her arm absentmindedly and droplets of blood sprang out as if by magic. Her skin was thin as paper.

"I will miss Stephanie's visits," she said, "I've missed seeing her."

Eduardo winced. "It is about Stephanie."

"Is she all right?" she asked sharply. "You must tell me. Is the earache worse?"

He said that Stephanie had flushed a live kitten down the toilet and he had no money to pay the plumber.

"You haven't the money to pay a plumber?" Lilly said, bewildered. She rubbed the blood into her arm. Gently, without looking at it, she smeared it into her skin.

Stephanie was playing with the kitten and the kitten nipped her or perhaps it was that the kitten took food from her plate and she was angry and wanted to punish it. "Of course there is no excuse for such a thing," Eduardo said. "She should not have done it. A very ugly thing to do. She does not have an earache, she is being punished. I wanted to spare your feelings. I know you are charmed by Stephanie. You do not want to know this."

"I must speak to her, Eduardo. You must bring her here and let me talk to her right away. Does she know this is wrong?"

"She says she is sorry," he said dismissively.

"She is so gentle," Lilly protested, "so respectful of everything, the books, the flowers. She fills Amiga's water dish. I find it difficult to believe she would do such harm."

"I knew you would not believe it," Eduardo said.

"I must see her. I will pay for the plumber. You must return as usual next week, every day, with Stephanie."

"I'm not asking for money. Sometimes you misunderstand me. But I must work digging a swimming pool for a month so that I can pay the plumber." He spoke stubbornly, as though spellbound.

"I will give you the money you need now. Please pay attention to what I am saying."

He nodded. "You're bleeding," he said.

.   .   .

Stephanie ran to Lilly and hugged her legs.

"Hello, dear," Lilly said, "my little dear."

The child giggled and clutched her. "I want to read, I want to color, I want to make those little cupcakes with the coconut."

"Stephanie, we must . . . Listen to me," Lilly said. "I want to ask you something."

"Sí," Stephanie said solemnly.

"The dress I gave you, why do you never wear it?" How shameful of me, Lilly thought, but I don't know how to begin. I am proceeding but I don't know how to begin. The child is slipping into the dark and no one knows, that dreadful Eduardo certainly doesn't know. He is concerned only with the cost to him! she thought with disgust. The cost of a plumber! While this child was slipping unconscious into the dark.

"My mama gave it to my sister. She said it was too big for me."

"And do you think it is too big?" Lilly said quietly, purposelessly.

"I'm sorry that the dress is not mine," Stephanie said.

"Do you know what it means to be sorry?" Lilly said in the same lazy, idle tone.

Stephanie patted Lilly's hands with her own small ones. "Could we color? Do you still have the crayons?"

"Do you want to draw?"

"No, color. There is a book you let me color in." She looked at Lilly worriedly. "Have you forgotten?"

They kept Stephanie's books and playthings in a bureau with a locking drawer. The key was on a ribbon on top of the bureau. The child liked the ceremony of unlocking the drawer. She liked the embroidered corners of the napkins they put on a pewter tray when they had lemonade.

"I have my own *hamaca* now," Stephanie said. "I do not have to sleep with my sister."

Danny walked past and smiled at them.

"What else has happened at your house?" Lilly asked. "You know I have not seen you for a long while. Have you been sick?"

"I am strong," Stephanie said, placing the books on a table and arranging the crayons in a pleasing fan shape. "I am never sick. Sometimes Mama is." She turned the pages of the coloring book. "That one is smudged," she said critically. "That was when I was a baby."

"Not so many weeks ago," Lilly said. "Why don't you color this page?"

"*Gatito,*" Stephanie said. "The kitten."

She set to work while Lilly watched her raptly. She was learning ignorance, Lilly marveled. She had begun to be false, false to herself and others. Lilly would not allow this, she would not. This was the child of whom Barbara had said, "Why, she thinks you hung the moon!" She had a responsibility to this child.

"Is that your kitten?" Lilly asked.

"*Sí.*" Stephanie was humming to herself. "He is black. He has white ears. He likes cupcakes." She selected another crayon. "I don't know. I don't really have a kitten. I have a *hamaca.*"

"Stephanie," Lilly said. She grasped the child's hands and held them fast. She felt them softly crumpling in her own. "You must not pretend this did not happen."

· · ·

Night. It was nothing if not reliable. Again, a single massed figure. A threat made material, followed by the ritual of crying out, the lamp rocking on the table as she fumbled for the switch, the little dog Amiga limping away, fearing her . . .

Instead, Lilly only gripped the sheets and, turning, pressed her face against the wall. Her eyes were wet. If it wasn't a dream, she reasoned, she wouldn't even feel it.

· · ·

It was time for a drink in the garden. She didn't drink wine because the sulfites were considered to be bad for her condition. She had a tequila over ice. She nibbled an almond. Eduardo sat comfortably with them, drinking from a bottle of Squirt.

"We're celebrating," Danny said. "Eduardo has bought a car—a VW one year younger than Eduardo."

"It is the first car in my family," Eduardo said gravely, without looking at Lilly. "No one in my family has ever had a car."

"We looked at eight before Eduardo decided," Danny said.

"You did all the paperwork," Eduardo said. "It was difficult paperwork."

"But it was you who made such a good down payment with your savings." Danny said to Lilly, "I told him we'd help him out with the rest."

"I will be working harder but that is only right," Eduardo said submissively.

"I can hardly see you working any harder than you do," Danny said.

"My first errand in my beautiful car was to take Stephanie home. We stopped for ice cream."

"She was terribly upset about something yesterday," Danny said. "What was that all about?"

Eduardo grimaced and squeezed his belly. "Stomachache."

"She's a sweet little girl," Danny said.

"Then I drove back in my fantastic car," Eduardo said. "That is when I bought the tequila. My gift."

"It's very smooth," Danny said.

Eduardo grinned. He was happy about the car. He was going to take good care of it.

CHARITY

THEY HAD BEEN told about it ecstatically by a police officer eating a tamale at a cafe near the Arizona/New Mexico border.

"I just went out there in all that white sand and got me a dune and went up on it and looked and looked and just let it sink in, and I never saw anything like it, never felt anything like it. I think I could stay out there in that white sand for a real long time and I don't know exactly why."

"It doesn't sound like something you'd want to do too often," Richard said. The policeman frowned. Then he ignored them.

Back in the car, Janice wanted to go there immediately. They were having a look at the Southwest on their way to Santa Fe. They were both wearing khaki suits, and Richard had a hand-painted tie he had paid a great deal of money for around his neck.

They drove to the White Sands National Monument, paid the admission and went in. The park ranger said, "We invite you to get out of your car and explore a bit, climb a dune for a better view of the endless sea of sand all around you."

They drove slowly along a loop road. Everything was white and orderly. It was as if the dunes had a sense of mission. Here and there, people were fervently throwing themselves down them and laughing.

"Do you want to get out?" Richard said. "I'll wait in the car."

Janice felt that she was still capable of awe and transfiguration and was uncomfortable when, together with Richard, she felt not much of anything. She was distracted with the knowledge that they were on a loop road. She studied the dunes without hope. As they were leaving, they saw something small and translucent, like a lizard, stagger beneath their wheels, and they both remarked on that.

"I don't know what that policeman was talking about," Richard said.

"He was trying to express something spiritual."

"Don't you get tired of that out here? Everything's sacred and mysterious and for the initiated only. Even the cops are after illumination. It wears me out, to be quite honest."

She wished she had gotten out of the car. She hadn't even gotten out of the car. She was wearing high heels. "Let's go back," she said. "Let's try it again."

"Janice," Richard said.

After some miles he said, "I forgot to take a leak back there."

"Really!" she exclaimed.

"I'm going to pull into this rest stop."

"To take a leak! How good!" she said. She fixed an enthralled expression upon him.

Outside, the heat was breathtaking and the desert had a slightly lavender cast. People were standing under a ramada, speaking loudly about family members who smoked like chimneys and lived into their nineties. Farther away, someone was calling to a small dog. "Peaches," they called, "you come here this instant." The dog seemed sincere in its unfamiliarity with the name Peaches. This was clearly a name the dog felt did not indicate its true nature, and it was not going to respond to it.

The road led past the toilets and ramadas through a portion of landscape where every form of plant life was explained with signs, then back out onto the highway. Janice walked along it toward a group of vending machines. She loved vending-machine coffee. She felt it had an unusual taste and wasn't for everyone. While waiting for the cardboard cup to sling itself down and fill with the uncanny liquid, she noticed a chalky purple van parked nearby. Two beautiful children stood beside it with their arms folded, looking around as though they had a certain amount of authority. They were rather dirty and were lanky and blond and striking. A man and woman were rummaging around inside the open van. Both the man and the boy were barefoot and shirtless. The woman, who had long, careless hair, said something to the girl, who climbed inside just as the man triumphantly produced what appeared to be an empty pizza box. Janice could hardly take her eyes off them. She finished the coffee, which was now cold and tasted even more peculiar, and returned to Richard and their rental car, which had a small scratch on the hood that she had taken great pains to point out to the agency so that they would not be held responsible for it. The grille had collected a number of butterflies. Without speaking, she got in and shut the door. She'd like to tell Richard how much she refrained from saying to him, but actually she refrained from saying very little.

As they passed the van, the man raised the scrap of box on which was now printed in crayon PLEASE: NEED GAS MONEY.

The colon in this plea touched Janice deeply. "Richard," she said, "we must give that family some money."

The man held the sign close to his chest, just above an appendectomy scar, as the children looked stonily into space.

"Richard!" she said.

"Oh, please, Janice," he said. "Honestly."

"Go back," she said.

They had reached the highway, and Richard accelerated. "Why do you always want to go back. We're not going back. Why don't you do things the first time?"

She gasped at the unfairness of this remark. She considered rearing back and hammering at the windshield with her high-heeled shoes. "I want to give that poor family some gas money," she said.

"Someone will give them money."

"But I want it to be us!"

Richard drove faster.

"Look," she said reasonably, "you drink a lot, Richard, you know you do. And what if you were in the hospital and you needed a new liver and the doctor finally came in and he said, 'I have good news, the hospital has found a liver for you.' Wouldn't you be grateful?"

"I would," Richard said thoughtfully.

"Someone would have given you a second chance."

"It would be a dead person," Richard said, still thoughtful. "It would have to have been."

"I wish I were driving," she said.

"Well, you're not."

Janice moaned. "I hate you," she said. "I do."

"Let's just get to Santa Fe," Richard said. "It's a civilized town. It will have a civilizing effect on us."

"That tie makes you look stupid," she said.

"I know," he said. He wrenched the knot free, rolled down the window and threw the tie out.

"What are you doing!" Janice cried. The tie was of genuine cellulose acetate and had been painted in the forties. It depicted a Plains Indian brave standing before a pueblo. That the scene was incorrect, that it had been conceived in utter ignorance, made it more expensive and, they were told, more valuable in the long run. But now there was no long run. The tie was toast. She shifted in her seat and stared breathlessly into the distance ahead. She thought of the little family with grave compassion.

"I'm afraid I have to stop again. For gas," he said.

He was pitiless, she thought. A moral aborigine. She hugged herself.

They rolled off an exit into a town that stretched a single block deep for miles along the highway and pulled into a gas station mocked up to look like a trading post, with a corral beside it filled with old, big-finned cars. Richard got out and pumped gas. Then he cleaned the windshield, grinning at her through the glass.

She did not know him, she thought. She was really no more acquainted with who he was than she was familiar with the cold dark-matter theory, say, or the origination of the universe.

He tapped on the glass. "Want to come inside?" he said. "Shot glasses, velvet paintings, lacquered scorpions?"

He was a snob, she thought.

He sighed and walked away, patting the breast pocket of his jacket for his wallet. Janice moved across the seat quickly, grasped the wheel and drove off in a great rattle and shriek of sand. She was back at the rest stop in fifteen minutes. The children had climbed the van's ladder and were lying on the roof. The woman was nowhere visible. The man was still rigidly holding the sign. Janice pulled up beside him.

"How you doing?" he said. He had bright, pale eyes.

"I want to give you twenty dollars," Janice said. She opened her purse and was disturbed to find she had only two fifty-dollar bills.

"Rose!" the man yelled, lowering the sign. He had a long, smooth torso, except for the appendectomy scar.

The woman emerged from the van and regarded Janice coolly.

"Yes?" she said.

"I saw your sign," Janice said, confused.

The children rose languidly from the roof and looked down at her.

"We have to travel seventy miles to our home and get these children in school tomorrow," Rose said formally. "What we do, what our policy is, is we drive to the nearest gas station and at that point you give us the amount you've decided on. That way you'll be assured that we're using it for gas and gas only."

Janice was grateful for the rules they had worked out.

"People will give you money at a rest stop whereas they wouldn't at a gas station," the man said. "It's just human nature. They're more at peace with themselves in rest stops."

"You can leave dogs and cats at rest stops and someone will pick them up," the boy said. "We left a couple of dogs here a couple weeks ago and they're gone now. Someone picked them up, gave them a good home."

Introductions were made. The man's name was Leo. The children were Zorro and ZoeBella. Janice identified herself too.

"Skinny Puppy's my gang name," Zorro said, "but use it at your peril."

"Gang name my ass," Leo said. "He doesn't know anything about gangs. He signed a lowrider last week. Practically got us killed."

"I didn't know I was signing," Zorro said. "I just had my hand out the window."

"Bastard about run us off the highway," Leo said.

Janice realized that she was gazing at them openly, a little stupidly. She suggested that they drive to the gas station so they could all be on their way.

"Can I go with you?" Rose asked. "I would like to feel like a human being, if only for a few miles."

"Lemme too!" Zorro cried. He opened the back door of Janice's car, tumbled over the front seat and snuggled against her. "Mnnnn, you smell fine," he said.

"I don't know where he picks that shit up from," Rose muttered. "Certainly not from his father. Get out of that vehicle now!" she screamed.

The child flipped backward over the seat and out the door and jumped into the van. ZoeBella, who had not uttered a word, climbed in beside him.

Janice invited Rose to ride with her to the gas station, which Leo seemed to be familiar with. She felt blessed with social responsibility. She was doing well. It would be over soon, and she would be able to look back on this in the future. Richard had only one mental key and it didn't open all locks, she had always felt this about Richard. And she had lots of mental keys, she thought gratefully, and that's why she was moving so freely through a world that welcomed her.

Leo started the van with difficulty. Blue smoke poured from the tailpipe.

"That doesn't look good," Janice noted.

"Rings, seals, valves, you name it," Rose said.

The van gained the highway and wobbled off ahead of them. Smoke appeared to be rising from the wheels as well. The sky was cloudless and sharply blue, and the smoke floundered upward into it.

"Some people like the sky out here," Rose volunteered, "but I prefer the sky over New York City. Now that's sky. The big buildings push it back so it's way, way overhead. It looks wilder that way."

Janice agreed, thinking that this was a highly original remark. She felt splendid about herself. She looked at Rose warmly.

"That Zorro smudged your seat," Rose said, regarding a dusty footprint on the car's upholstery.

Janice waved this concern away. "Such beautiful children," she said. "And such unusual names."

"God knows I didn't want to call him Zorro, but his father insisted. Those two aren't from the same stock. ZoeBella's dad Warren was blind. I hope that you, like many others, aren't under the misperception that blind people are good people. It just isn't so. Blind people don't feel that they have to interact with others at all. They contribute nothing to a conversation. He had a wonderful dog, though, Mountain. Mountain came to Lamaze class with us. Lamaze encourages you to focus on something other than birth and I focused on Mountain week after week, but when it was finally time to have ZoeBella they wouldn't let Mountain into the delivery room. A violation of infection-control procedures, they said. Well, I freaked, and I think the whole thing messed up ZoeBella too. Here I went the whole pregnancy with no cigarettes or liquor and then they won't let the goddamn dog into the delivery room. It was a very, very difficult birth and Warren, the bastard, was no help at all. But we sued the hospital for not letting us have Mountain in there, and they settled out of court. Warren was long gone by then, but that money did us for four years, Leo and Zorro too. What an inspiration that was. I wish I could come up with another one that good. Have you ever fucked a blind man?"

"Why, no," Janice said. "No, I haven't."

"Do it before you die, girl," Rose said. "There's nothing like it."

Janice nodded.

"But don't stick around afterwards. Get your cookies out of there," Rose advised.

Janice nodded again. She was beginning to worry somewhat about Richard's mood when she retrieved him. The van weaved smoldering before them. Janice felt a little queasy watching it. By the time they reached the exit, Janice found that she was gripping the steering wheel tightly. The van turned not into the gas station where Janice had left Richard but into one across the street, where it clattered to a stop.

"Makes you want a cocktail just looking at that heap, doesn't it?" Rose said.

"I'd like to give you fifty dollars, if you don't mind," Janice said. "I think you probably need some oil too. Wouldn't you like some oil? To make it all the way home?"

"Oh, you could drop a bundle into that thing," Rose said. "It's a suckhole." She accepted the bill slowly from Janice's fingers. "Thank you," she said slowly. She seemed absorbed in some involuted ritual. She didn't respect the money, it was clear, but she respected the person who gave her the money. Was that it? Janice wondered. Why was she giving her so much money anyway? Her own behavior was becoming increasingly suspect.

Rose got out of the car, stretched and ambled toward her family. Janice drove across the street. The trading post was locked tight. Four spotted dogs with heads the size of gallon buckets regarded her avidly from the car corral.

"Richard!" she called. The dogs went into an uproar. They raced around the enclosure, baying with the thrill of duty, upsetting their water dishes. Janice drove slowly in circles in the area of the trading post, then pulled out into the street and came to the end of town. The town simply stopped at an enormous Road Runner statue, beyond which were many thousands of acres of grazing land with not a creature grazing. Richard was a wily and annoying adversary, Janice thought. She stopped the car near the statue and got out, taking tiny sips of the superheated air, afraid to breathe too deeply. An elderly couple approached and asked if she would take a picture of them with their camera.

"Doesn't it have one of those timers?" Janice said. "Can't you place it on a rock, set the timer and have it take its own picture?"

The old couple looked puzzled and began to tremble.

"OK. Forgive me," Janice said. "I'm sorry. Give it here."

"Be sure to get it all in," the woman said. "You have to back up."

Janice backed up and raised the camera to her eye. They were there.

"You have to step back some still," the woman said.

Janice moved farther back and clipped the side of her shoe against a trash can.

"That must be why they put that receptacle there," the woman said.

"The receptacle marks the spot!" her withered companion shouted.

"Smile if you want to," Janice said. "Done. Got it." She had not taken the picture. She would not. It was a defensible right.

"Thank you so much," the old man said.

"Most kind of you," the woman said, "once you agreed."

Janice returned to the car on her broken heel and drove back through the town, honking her horn frequently. Richard was not only wily and annoying, he could be actually hazardous. His behavior was hazardous, she thought. She circled the pumps of the deserted trading post once again. The big-headed dogs were lying on their stomachs, sharing something fuscous and eviscerated. She drove across the street. Rose and the children were sitting on the ground on a bedsheet. The van was on a lift inside the garage.

"Are you looking for someone?" Rose asked.

"No," Janice said. "I don't look as though I am, do I?"

"You look hungry, then, or something," Rose said.

"I'm hungry," Zorro said. "Jesus I am."

"Are those horse?" ZoeBella said, pointing at Janice's shoes.

Janice was startled to hear her voice, which was soft and solemn. "What?" she said.

"Your shoes, are they horse?"

"I don't know. They're leather of some sort. That would be awful, I guess, if they were, wouldn't it?"

"You seem uncertain," ZoeBella said quietly.

Leo came up to them, wiping his greasy hands on his pants. Stripes of grease ran down his chest and there was oil in his hair. "We got a little problem here but it can be fixed," he said. "Man here's going to let me use his tools. Why don't you women and children get something to eat," he said expansively. "Sit in a nice air-conditioned restaurant and get something nice to eat."

Rose was particular about the restaurant. She wanted it dark, with booths, no salad bar, no view of the outside. They got into Janice's car and drove up the street again. Zorro was sent into several establishments to determine their suitability. He had put on a T-shirt that said BAN LEG-HOLD TRAPS. A number of birds and animals crippled and quite conceivably dead were arranged colorfully around a frightful black iron trap.

"He loves that shirt, but I don't think he gets it," Rose confided to Janice.

"You should bury that shirt, with Zorro in it," ZoeBella said quietly.

Janice continued to scan the street for Richard. She saw no one who even remotely resembled him, not that she would have settled for that, of course.

"You sure you're not looking for someone?" Rose asked.

"Not at all," Janice said. "I'm just trying to be aware of my surroundings."

ZoeBella leaned over the front seat and said softly, "I think that policeman behind us wants you to pull over."

"Yes!" Zorro said. "There go the misery lights!"

Janice was told by the officer that she had drifted through a stop sign. He very much resembled the officer she and Richard had encountered at breakfast. While he was writing out the ticket, which was for two hundred dollars, Rose asked him which eating establishment he would recommend, and he recommended the one they were parked in front of.

"This kind of event calls for a cocktail," Rose said to Janice. "It always does."

Inside, Janice felt disoriented. ZoeBella placed her small hand in Janice's and led her to a booth. They sat holding hands opposite Zorro, whose T-shirt featured prominently in the darkness. Janice ordered a double gin with ice and Rose specified an imported bottled beer, then ordered turkey plates for everyone.

"Turkey plate's always the best," she said.

ZoeBella did not release Janice's hand even after the food arrived. The children ate as though starved.

"Do you believe in God?" ZoeBella murmured.

Janice was trying to locate a hair which had found its way onto her tongue.

Rose said, "When I was ZoeBella's age, every time I thought of God I saw him as something in a black Speedo bathing suit and I saw myself sitting on his lap, but this perception was drummed out of me. Just drummed out. Now whenever the name comes up I don't think anything."

"I think of God as a magician," ZoeBella whispered, looking closely at Janice. "A rich magician who has a great many sheep who he hypnotizes so he won't have to pay for shepherds or fences to keep them from running away. The sheep know that eventually the magician wants to kill them because he wants their flesh and their skin. So first the magician hypnotizes them into thinking that they're immortal and that no harm is being done to them when they get skinned, that on the contrary it will be very good for them and even pleasant. Then he hypnotizes them into thinking that the magician is their good master who loves them. Then he hypnotizes them into thinking that they're not sheep at all. And after all this, they never run away but quietly wait until the magician requires their flesh and their skin."

ZoeBella's skin was very pale and her eyes were large and blue. "Goodness," Janice said, perturbed. Only a piece of bread was going to find this hair, she decided. She pushed one into her mouth.

Zorro said, "I think of God—"

His mother yanked his arm sharply. "We don't want to hear that again," she said.

Zorro collected everyone's forks and put them in the pocket of his shorts.

"We always need forks," Rose explained to Janice. "I don't know what happens to them at our house."

The children ordered large butterscotch sundaes and polished them off within minutes. ZoeBella ate delicately but with lightning speed. She had released Janice's hand to better wield the long spoon, but when she finished she tucked her hand in Janice's once again.

"I hope I'm at school tomorrow," she said in her almost inaudible voice. "If I'm not at school tomorrow I don't know what I'll do." She arranged her face in an expression of horror.

Janice couldn't imagine a child like ZoeBella thriving at school, but she squeezed the child's sticky hand. The magician and the sheep had caused her to feel a little unwell and considerably undirected, though she now knew what she would do.

She would take Rose and the children to their home. She was sure that the situation with Leo and the van had not improved and she was eager to finish what she had begun. Otherwise, in what way would she be able to think about it? She wouldn't be able to think about it. They lived in a town that was not exactly on the way to Santa Fe, but she could still make it to Santa Fe before dark if they left immediately. Richard had made reservations at a hotel there. There would possibly be a message waiting, or even Richard himself. If there wasn't, if he wasn't, then when she arrived she would be the message. One's life after all is the message, isn't it, the way one lives one's life, the good one carries out?

"I can see you're thinking," ZoeBella said in a quiet, disappointed voice.

Back at the garage, Leo was agreeable to Janice's idea. "I believe I'm going to be here for days," he said. He kissed the children and shook Janice's hand. In the car again, Janice remarked that Leo seemed like a good man.

"He's all right," Rose said. "Whenever he gets drunk he threatens to kill the kids' rabbits, but he hasn't done it yet."

They drove in silence for a while. When they got to their home, Janice was not going to go inside. She would be invited, but under no circumstance would she go inside. She didn't want to go so far as to enter that home even in her thoughts. She would leave them at their own threshold and be gone.

"What's your credit card look like?" Zorro asked. "Is it black with a mountain on it and an eagle and a big orange sun? Because if it is, you left it back there by the cash register. I saw it when I got the toothpicks."

"Zorro sees credit cards everywhere," Rose said. "I've told him never never pick them up. He's got a shrewd eye, and I want him to have a shrewd eye, but my feeling is that he could go from shrewd to dishonest real quick."

"I'm not going back," Janice said.

No one contested this. They were on a narrow blacktop road streaking urgently through the desert. There were a few scattered adobes framed by enormous prickly pear cactus, their red fruits glowing in the late-afternoon light. A man was riding a horse bareback in a field.

"There is a horse," ZoeBella said reverently.

Then Zorro saw the snake on the edge of the asphalt.

"Lookitim!" he screamed. "Lookit the size of that sucker! He's a miracle, you can't just pass him by!"

He grabbed the wheel and turned it toward the snake, but Janice wrenched it back and slammed on the brakes. The car shot off the road, not quite clearing a stony wash, and with a snapping of axles it crumpled against a patch pocket of wild-flowers—primrose and sand verbena and, as ZoeBella pointed out quietly later, sacred datura, a plant of which every part was poisonous.

"Is everyone all right?" Rose said. "All in one piece? That's the important thing, nothing else matters."

"I just wanted that snake so bad," Zorro said.

"He's always after his dad to hit things for him," Rose said. "You're in somebody else's vehicle, Zorro! You are a guest in another person's car!"

They got out of the car with difficulty and looked at it. It was clearly a total wreck. The key had snapped off in the ignition, so Janice couldn't even unlock the trunk to retrieve her suitcase.

ZoeBella touched Janice's hand. "I'm glad you didn't run over the snake," she whispered.

"I have a terrible headache," Janice said.

"You bumped your head pretty bad," Rose agreed. "I saw a motel back there. Why don't we get a room and declare this day over."

There was only one room available at the motel, and there was a lone, large bed which pretty much filled it. The other rooms were unoccupied, according to the Indian girl in the office, but each possessed a unique incapacity disqualifying it from use. A clogged drain, a charred carpet, a cracked toilet, a staved-in door. Fleas.

Zorro soared from the door to the bed and began bouncing on it. "Skinny Puppy enters the ring!" he shouted. He crouched and weaved, jabbing the air. Rose swatted him away.

"You lie down," she instructed Janice. "I'll take the kids over to the cafe so you can rest. They've got cocktails, I noticed. Do you want me to bring you back a cocktail?"

"I think I'll just lie down," Janice said.

"Don't do anything until you've rested a bit," Rose said.

"Don't look in the mirror or anything," ZoeBella urged her softly.

"You look white as a sheet," Rose said. "Maybe we should stay with you just until you get your color back."

"I don't feel at all well," Janice said. She crept across the bed and lay on her back. She didn't want to close her eyes.

"Scootch over just a little bit," Rose said, "more to the middle so we can all fit."

They all lay on the bed. After a few moments someone began to snore. Janice wouldn't want to bet her last fifty it wasn't her.

ACK

We were visiting friends of mine on Nantucket. Over the years they've become more solitary. They're quite a bit older than we are, lean, intelligent and carelessly stylish. They drink too much. And I drink too much when I visit them. Sometimes we'd just eat cereal for supper; other times we'd be subjected to an entire stuffed fish and afterwards a tray of Grape-Nut pudding. Their house is old and uncomfortable, with a small yard, dark with hydrangeas in August. This was August. I told my wife not to expect dinner from my erratic friends, Betty and Bruce. We would have a few drinks, then return to the inn where we were staying and have a late supper. Only one other guest was expected this evening, a local woman who had ten daughters.

"What an awful lot," my wife said.

"I'm sure we'll hear about them," I said.

"I suppose so," Bruce said, struggling to open an

institutional-size jar of mayonnaise that had been set on a weathered picnic table in the yard.

"She's unlikely to talk about much else with that many," my wife said. "Are any of them strange?"

"One's dead, I believe," our host said, still struggling with the jar. "'Whatsoever thy hand findeth to do, do it with all thy might . . .'" he said, addressing his own exertions.

"Let me give that a try," I said, but Bruce had finally broken the plastic seal.

"I meant strange as in intellectually or emotionally or physically challenged," my wife said. She had already decided to dislike this poor mother.

Bruce dipped a slice of wilted carrot into the jar. "I really like mayonnaise; do you, Paula? I can't remember."

"Bruce, you know very well it's Pauline," Betty said.

"I'm addicted to mayonnaise, practically," Bruce said.

My wife smiled and shook her head. If she had resolved to become relaxed in that moment it would be a great relief, for Bruce had been kind to me and there was no need for tension between them. Pauline prefers to be in control of our life and our friendships. She's a handsome woman, canny and direct, never unreasonable. I suppose some might find her cold but I am in thrall to her because I had almost been crushed by life. I had some rough years before Pauline, years I only just managed to live through. I might as well have been stumbling about in one of those great whiteouts that occur in the far north where it is impossible to distinguish between a small object nearby and a large object a long way off. In whiteouts there is no certainty and every instinct is betrayed—even the birds fly into the ground, believing it to be air, and perish. I strained to see and could not, and torn by strange sorrows and shames, I twice attempted suicide. But then a calm overtook me, as though my mind had taken pity on me and called off the hopeless search I had undertaken. I was thirty-two then. I met Pauline the following year and she accepted me, broken and wearied as I was, with an assurance that further strengthened me. We have a lovely home outside Washington. She wants a child, which I am resisting.

We were all smiling at the mayonnaise jar as though it were one of the sweet night's treasures when a bell jangled on a rusted chain wrapped around the garden gate. We had likewise engaged the same bell an hour before. A woman appeared, thinner than I expected, almost gaunt, and shabbily dressed. She seemed a typical wellborn island eccentric, and looked at us boldly and disinterestedly . . . It was difficult to determine her age and thus impossible to guess at the ages of her many daughters. My first impression was that none of them had accompanied her.

"Starky! Have a drink, my girl!" Bruce said in greeting.

She embraced him, resting her cheek for a moment in his hair, which was long and reached the collar of his checkered shirt. She breathed in the smell of his hair much as I had and found it, I could imagine, sour but strangely satisfying. She then turned to Betty and kissed, as I had, her soft warm cheek.

She had brought a gift of candles, which Betty found holders for. The candles were lit and Pauline admired the pleasant effect, for with night, the hydrangeas had cast an almost debilitating gloom over the little garden. It did not trouble me that we had brought nothing. We had considered a pie but the prices had offended us. It was foolish to spend so much money on a pie.

"Guinivere," Bruce called. "We're so glad you came!"

A figure moved awkwardly toward us and sat down heavily. It was a young woman with a flat round face. Everything about her seemed round. Her mouth at rest was small and round.

"Look at all that mayonnaise," Starky said. "Bruce remembered it's a favorite of yours."

"I like maraschino cherries now," the girl said.

"Yes, she's gone on to cherries," her mother said.

"I have jars of them awaiting fall's Manhattans," Bruce assured her. "Retrieve them from the pantry, dear. They're in the cabinet by the waffle iron."

"Guinivere is a pretty name," my wife said.

"She was instrumental in saving the whales last week," her mother said. "The first time, not when they beached themselves again. The photographer was there from the paper but he always excludes Guinivere, she doesn't photograph well."

Every year brings the summertime tragedy of schools of whales grounding on the shore. It's their fidelity to one another that dooms them, as well as their memories of earlier safe passage. They return to a once navigable inlet and find it a deadly maze of unfamiliar shoal. The sound of their voices—the clicks and cries quite audible to their would-be rescuers—is heartbreaking, apparently.

Pauline pointed out that those sounds would seem that way only to sympathetic ears. It was simply a matter of our changing attitudes toward them, she argued. Nantucket's wealth was built on the harpooning of the great whales. Had they not cried out then with the same anguished song?

Starky murmured liltingly, *"Je t'aimerai toujours bien que je ne t'ai jamais aimé."*

It was impossible to tell if she possessed an engaging voice or not, the song, or rather this fragment, being so brief. It was quite irrelevant, in my opinion, to the topic of whales.

Pauline frowned. "I will always love you though I never loved you? Is that it? Certainly isn't much, is it?"

"One of Starky's daughters has a wonderful voice," Betty said, looking about distractedly.

Pauline nudged me as if to say, Here it's beginning and now we'll have to hear about all of them, even the dead one. She then continued resolutely, "As a statement of devotion, I mean. But perhaps it was taken out of context?"

"Everything's context," Bruce said, "or is as I grow older."

Guinivere returned with a bottle of cherries and munched them one by one, dipping her fingers with increasing difficulty into the narrow jar.

"Those aren't good for you," Pauline said.

The girl tipped the liquid from the jar onto the flagstones and retrieved the last of the cherries.

"They're very bad for you," Pauline counseled. "They're not good for anyone."

The girl ignored her.

"Guinivere has a job," Betty said. "She works at the library. She puts all the books back in their proper places—don't you, Guinivere?"

"Someone has to do the lovely things," Bruce said.

"And someone does the ugly things too," Guinivere said without humor. "In Amarillo, Texas, more cattle have been slaughtered than any other place in the world. They make nuclear bombs in Amarillo as well."

"You must read the books then," Pauline asked, "as you put them back on the shelves?" Her efforts at engagement with this unfortunate child were making me uncomfortable. She wanted a child, but of course a lovely one. She had no doubt it would be lovely. Would even a bird build its nest if it did not have the instinct for confidence in the world?

"I have a joke," Guinivere said. "It's for him." She pointed at me. "They name roads for people like you." She paused. "One Way," she said, and she smiled a round smile. She was much older than I initially though.

"You're such a chatterbox tonight," her mother said. "You must let others speak."

Guinivere immediately fell silent, and for a moment we all were silent.

"I'm going to get more ice," Pauline announced.

"Thank you!" Bruce said. "And more ingredients for the rickeys all around, if you please."

Starky rose to accompany her into the house, which I knew would vex Pauline as she wanted only to remove herself from this group for a while, a group I'm sure she found most unpromising.

"You look good, my boy," Bruce said.

"Thank you, it's Pauline," I said. Betty's look was skeptical. "I've found there's a trick to knowing where you are," I said. "It's knowing where you were five minutes ago."

"Why, you were here!" Betty said.

"I know where you were long before five minutes ago," Bruce said.

"Yes, you do," I agreed. "And if that man, that man you knew, came into the garden right now and sat down with us, I wouldn't recognize him."

"You wouldn't know what to say to him?" Bruce asked.

"I could be of no help to him."

"Those were dark times for you."

I shrugged. I had once wanted to kill myself and now I did not. The thoughts I harbored then lack all reality for me.

Quiet voices from the street drifted toward us. The tourists were "laning," a refined way of saying they were peering into the lamplit and formal rooms of other people's houses and commenting on the furnishings, the paintings, the flower arrangements and so on.

My thoughts returned to the whales and their deaths. They were small pilot whales, not the massive sperm whales Pauline had made reference to, the taking of which had made this island renowned. The pilot whales hadn't wished to kill themselves, of course. But one was in distress, the one first to realize the gravity of the situation, the dangerous imminence of an unendurable stranding, and the others were caught up in the same incomprehension. In the end they had no choice but to go where the dying one was going.

Or that's one way of putting it. A marine biologist would know far better than me.

Pauline returned carrying a tray with an assortment of bottles and a plastic bowl of melting ice. "Starky is on the phone," she announced.

"It's probably her real estate agent," Bruce said. "She told me he might be contacting her tonight. She's selling her home, the one where she raised all her girls."

"I'm sure she'll get whatever he's asking," Pauline said. "People are mad for this place, aren't they? They'll pay any price to say they have a home here."

The night was growing colder. Bruce had brought out several old sweaters, and I pulled one over my head. It fit well enough—a murrey cashmere riddled with moth holes.

Betty placed her tanned and deeply wrinkled hand on mine. The veins were so close to the surface I wondered that they didn't alarm her whenever they caught her eye. She had to look at them sometimes.

"We are all of us unique, aren't we? And misunderstood," she said.

"No," I replied, not unkindly, for I was devoted to Betty, though I was beginning to wonder if she wasn't becoming a bit foolish with age. The world does not distinguish one grief from another. It is the temptation to believe otherwise that keeps us in chains. "We are not as dissimilar from one another as we prefer to think," I said.

The rickeys were not as refreshing as they had been earlier, perhaps because of the ice.

Starky reappeared, as gaunt and unexceptional as before and giving no explanation for what had become a prolonged absence.

"Oh, do begin now," Betty said.

"Begin what?" Pauline asked.

"Without further preamble?" Starky said.

"Or delay," Bruce said.

"What must this place be like in the winter!" Pauline exclaimed.

We all laughed, none more forgivingly than Starky, who then began, as I had suspected, to describe her children.

"My first daughter is neither bold nor innovative but feels a tenderness toward all things. When she was young she was understandably avaricious out of puzzlement and boredom, but experience has made her meek and devoted. She is loyal to my needs and outwardly appears to be the most praiseworthy of my children. She ensures that my lucky dress is always freshly cleaned and pressed and waiting for me on its cloth-covered hanger. Despite such conscientiousness, I feel most distanced from this child and might neglect her utterly were she not the first.

"My second daughter is the traveler of the family even though she seldom rises from her bed. One need only show her the shell of a queen conch or a paperweight with its glass enclosing a Welsh thistle and she is swimming in the Bahamas or tramping the British Isles, though this only in her mind for she is far too excitable and shy to make the actual journey. She prepares for her adventures by anticipating the worst, and when this does not occur she delights in her good fortune. Some who know her find her pitiful but I believe she has saved herself by her ingenuity. The bruises she shows me on her thin arms and legs, even on her dear face, incurred in the course of these travels, evoke my every sympathy."

"How preposterous," Pauline whispered to me.

"My third daughter," Starky continued, pausing to sip her drink, "is plain and compliant with great physical stamina. In fact it is by her strength that she attempts to atone for everything. She is sentimental and nostalgic, which is understandable for given her nature her future will be little different from her past. She is not lazy, on the contrary she labors hard and conscientiously, but her work is taken for granted. She is hopeful and trusts everyone, leaving herself open to betrayal. She pores over my trinkets, believing that they have special import for her. She often cries out for me in the night. She fears death more than I do, more, perhaps, than any of us here."

"Bless her heart," Betty said.

"Does she?" Pauline asked. "But there's no way of judging that, is there? I mean, how can you even presume—"

"I wish you'd continue," Betty said to Starky.

"Yes," Bruce said. "Mustn't get stalled on that one."

"My fourth daughter is a singer, an exquisite mezzo-soprano. Her voice was a great gift, she hasn't had a single lesson. Even when it became clear that she was extraordinary we decided against formal training, which would only have perverted her voice's singularity and freshness. Sing, I urged her always. Sing! For your voice will desert you one day without warning."

"Mommy," Guinivere said, startling me for I had forgotten her completely.

"Do sing for us, Guinivere," Betty said. "We so love it when you sing."

"Yes, go ahead," her mother said.

The girl's round mouth grew rounder still and after a moment in which, I suppose, she composed herself, she sang in the most thrilling voice:

> If there had anywhere appeared in space
> Another place of refuge, where to flee
> Our hearts had taken refuge in that place
> And not with thee
> And only when we found in earth and air,
> In heaven or hell, that such might nowhere be
> That we could not flee from thee anywhere,
> We fled to thee.

"How sweet," Pauline allowed.

"Is that Trench?" Bruce asked. "I'm not as keen as I used to be in identifying those old English hymnists."

Guinivere rose and said something urgently to Betty.

"Go behind the bushes, dear," Betty said. "It's quite all right."

"Behind the bushes!" Pauline appeared scandalized. "She's a grown woman!"

"Guinivere doesn't like our bathroom," Betty said. "It frightens her."

"Perhaps there are ghosts," Pauline said. She giggled and whispered in my ear, "Don't tell me the Vineyard wouldn't be better than this."

"I don't know about ghosts," Betty said, "but in any old house you can be sure things happened, cruel and desperate things."

When Guinivere had disappeared behind the large lavender globes of the hydrangeas, her mother said quietly, "Her voice is in decline."

"I find that difficult to believe," I said, though of course I am no expert. "Her voice is splendid."

Starky said calmly, "She is like a great tree in winter whose roots are cut, only mimicking what the other trees can promise—the life to come."

Guinivere returned and took her place. She could not be persuaded to sing again. We were all sitting on old metal chairs, rusted from years of the island's heavy, almost unremitting fog, but not so badly that they marked one's clothes. I believe Bruce and Betty stored them in the cellar during the winter.

"My fifth daughter," Starky resumed to my dismay, "is the one I personally taught about time. I did her no service for she is my most melancholy child. She is unable to give value to things and never surrenders herself to comforting distractions. Alternatives are meaningless to her. She is a hounded girl, desolate, a captive, seeking in silence some language that might serve her. Faith would allow her some relief but she resists the slavishness of spirit that faith would entail. No, for her faith is out of the question."

Bruce gestured for me to make fresh drinks for all. I wanted further drink badly, indeed I had almost taken Pauline's glass and drained it as my own. I made the drinks quickly, without the niceties of sugar or lime and with the last of the ice.

"My sixth daughter is dead," Starky said. "She ran the brief race prescribed to her and now her race is done."

"She has a lovely stone," Betty said.

"She wanted a stone," Starky said. "I had to assure her over and over that there would be a stone."

"Well, it's lovely," Betty said.

"She found the peace which the world cannot give," Starky said, quite unnecessarily, I thought.

Pauline stared at her, then turned to me and said, "What could she possibly mean? How could she know what the poor thing found?"

I wanted to calm her though I knew she was more angry than anxious. Only hours before this mad evening had begun we were sitting quite contentedly alone on the moors, or what on this island they refer to as moors. We had wasted the morning, we'd agreed then, but not the afternoon. We could not see the sea, though we were aware of it because of course it was all around us. Love's bright mother from the ocean sprung, the Greeks believed.

"I can't bear this another moment," Pauline said, rising to her feet. "Why do you expect to be so indulged? Why did you have so many? Where is the father? Who is the father? The children are freakish the way you present them. Why do you put them on such cruel display? Why are their efforts so feeble and familiar? Why are you not more concerned? This is not the way friends spend a sociable evening. Why didn't you tell a real story, not even once? How could you believe we would even be interested? No, I can't endure this any longer."

And with this she hurried out, unerringly I must say, through the dark garden, across the uneven flagstone. It took me several minutes to deliver my apologies and good-byes, but even so I left in such haste that it was not until I was well down the street that I realized I was still wearing Bruce's old sweater. I would mail it to him in the morning before we boarded the ferry. I wondered if Betty and Bruce would store the old chairs when the days grew bitter and if, assuming they did, the effort would be made to bring them out again in the spring.

It must have been quite late for the streets were deserted. I hoped that a walk, at my own pace in the light chill fog, would clear my head. Starky had seemed amused by Pauline's outburst and Betty and Bruce unperturbed, while Guinivere had not raised her head, either then or at my own departure. Indeed, she appeared to be practically in a stupor. Her mother might have been correct. The effort she was making could not be sustained much longer.

I walked slowly down the cobblestoned main street, turning left at the museum where earlier in the day Pauline and I had spent less than an hour for it was a dispiriting place, cheerfully staffed by volunteer docents but displaying the most grotesque weapons and tools of eighteenth-century whaling— knives and spades and chisels, harpoons and lances and fluke chains. Antique drawings and prints accompanied by descriptive commentary filled the walls. One phrase concerning the end of the flensing process, which took place alongside the ships, remains with me: *Finally the body was cast off and allowed to float away.* Most disturbingly put, I felt, the word *allowed* being particularly horrible.

Pauline had been quite right about the whales. Had they not cried out in the days of their destruction with exquisite and anguished song? Yet their pursuers, with a purpose unfathomable, wanted only to extinguish them. Indeed, man had reveled in the fine red mist that fell, as though from heaven, from the great collapsing hearts to herald the harried and bewildered creatures' deaths.

The inn where we had taken lodging was now in sight. I thought once again of the debt I owe Pauline. I owe her everything I am. I would even prefer that she would leave this life, in time, before me, though I do not feel strongly about this. Even so, it is proof of her success with me that I could entertain such a thought. One of us will be first, in any case, and until then, we have each other.

HAMMER

ANGELA HAD ONLY one child, a daughter who abhorred her. Darleen was now sixteen years old, a junior in boarding school who excelled in all her courses. Her dislike of Angela had become pronounced around the age of eleven, increasing in theatricality and studied venom until it leveled off in her thirteenth year, the year she went off to Mount Hastings.

Darleen's father had died in a scuba accident when she was but an infant. He had held his breath coming up the last twenty feet of an otherwise deep and successful dive. An absolute no-no. One did not hold one's breath on the ascent to the light no matter how eager one was to return. He had been instructed in that, as had Angela and everyone else in the resort training course they'd been taking. While he'd been recklessly rising Angela had still been fooling around down in the depths, interesting herself in a rock that was in the process of being dismantled or constructed—it was hard to tell which—by colorful wrasses.

Angela had known few men after her impetuous young husband, whose name had been Bruce. She lived in the house she had returned to as a widow in the town she'd always lived in. Despite the dislike her daughter felt toward her, Angela was devoted to Darleen and awaited the day when their estrangement would be over, for surely that day would come. At the same time she feared that something would break then in Darleen, never to be made good again.

Ever since the girl insisted on going off to boarding school, Angela had worked as a masseuse in an old spa on the outskirts of town. She found the work distasteful and yet persisted in it, kneading and pummeling, rapping and slapping, the trusting hides presented to her. The old bodies became delusionarily flattered and freshened beneath her cool hands. Still, she was not as popular as the other masseuses. She spoke little and had no regulars. In her white cubicle on a white wooden table beside the high white-sheeted table was an envelope with her name written on it, a reminder that a gratuity would be appreciated. Seldom did it contain anything at the end of the day, though once an extraordinarily long and vigorously curling eyebrow hair had been deposited there.

On a cold morning in late February, Angela had a single appointment. She knew the woman, a wealthy and opinionated patron of the arts who was dedicated to social inclusion, moral betterment, sculpture in the parks and dance. She smiled at Angela thinly, disappointed that she was not being served by Margaret, everyone's favorite. Outside the sky was dark, almost cyclonic, but inside a warm, optimistic light bathed everything. There was an orange on the table which really ought to be thrown out, and Angela left the room for a moment to dispose of it.

Midway through the session, just as Angela's tape was about to end—it was Schweitzer playing Bach's Fugue in G Minor, and she was dreamily placing the shaggy-haired theologian thumping away on an organ in the jungle, pulling out all the stops in a green and unreconciled jungle, which he was not doing at all of course—she snapped her prosperous client's wrist bone, and before the ambulance arrived she'd been fired.

"I have no choice, Angela," the manager said.

"What if the others signed a petition to keep me on?" Angela asked.

"They wouldn't do that, Angela. They wouldn't trouble themselves, you know that."

"Oh, it doesn't matter," Angela said.

"Of course it doesn't," he said.

Angela did not return home that night. Instead, she drove to the coast several hours away and boarded a ferry that served a number of weedy, unremarkable islands that were popular with the very rich, who maintained large and hidden homes there. In the tiny lounge of the ferry, people were talking about a dog that had fallen overboard during the previous night's crossing and had not yet been found. It was a chocolate-colored Lab named Turner. The owners, a young couple just married, were practically keening with distress, according to the purser. Angela stared at the water with the four other passengers. Occasionally, the ferry's searchlight would cast a broad beam over the waves.

Angela checked into the inn closest to the ferry slip on the first island. She had come here before in times of distress, usually when she was trying to stop drinking. The following day, in her old wool coat and with a borrowed scarf over her head, she walked along the beach. The few people she encountered referred to the drizzle as mizzle, which had been more or less constant since New Year's Day. Angela's thoughts floated beside her. The vigorous eyebrow hair in the envelope appeared more than once, seemingly determined to show its jurisdiction over her most recent months. It had quite attached itself to Angela, though only in spirit, for she certainly hadn't kept the damn thing.

When she boarded the ferry the next morning, people were talking about the brown Lab that had been rescued the night before, on the boat's last run. He'd actually slipped below the waves just before they'd got a flotation ring around him. He was an instant from being gone but they'd hauled him in, and he'd smiled the way Labs do, pulling back his lips in a black, rubbery grin. After he'd been warmed and fed, the distraught couple had been called, and when the ferry returned to the mainland the three of them were reunited. But the couple said it wasn't Turner. In their minds they had endured with Turner the weight of the stinging sea, the whipping of the starless dark, the bewilderment and despair that this animal too must surely have suffered. But this was not their Turner, and they were not going to take him home with them.

"I never saw a dog looked more like another dog in my life then," the cashier in the galley was saying. "That Turner came in here three days ago with those people and he ate a fried egg sandwich."

The couple apparently had been heckled off the boat.

"They weren't crying anymore," the cashier said. "They were stubborn about it, they'd made up their minds. It was the captain took the dog."

Angela pressed herself against the rail and looked at the water in much the same way she had earlier, waiting for something to appear. This time she would be the first to glimpse it. There! she imagined herself calling out to the others. Though it was unlikely now. No, it would never happen now.

She drove home, detouring through the grounds of the old spa, which looked as ruined and complacent as it had when it was a big part of Angela's life. Smoke rose from one of the chimneys. The fireplace in the game room frequently harbored a meager fire. The immense moribund pines, dying because of the town's controversial road-salting practices, loomed protectively over the winding narrow road.

The phone was ringing as she opened the door. It was Darleen, who announced that she was arriving the next day for a brief visit.

"It would be thoughtful of you if you canceled your appointments at that vile place you work so we could spend some time together," Darleen said.

"What would you like to do?" Angela said.

"I thought I'd help you put in a garden, Mummy."

"I don't have a garden, dear. There was never . . . I mean nothing's changed much since you were here last."

"I know the conditions under which you live, Mummy. I was just being annoying."

"How is school?"

"They've completed the new library, and we're allowed two days off from classes to move the books from the old institution down the hill to the new institution. We are to be utilized as a merry and willing human chain. I resist being so utilized. I'm here to learn."

"So you're coming here instead," Angela said. There was silence.

"Which is wonderful," Angela said. "Really wonderful."

"I'm hanging up, Mummy. You can continue with your inanities if you wish."

That night Angela had a dream. She was in a furniture store and the salesman was speaking about the wood of a bed she was looking at. Angela was not really interested in the bed and had no intention of buying it but she had been staring at it for some time. No wonder the salesman thinks I'm interested in it, she thought in her dream, I keep walking around and around it. Now some people, the salesman said, they look at a thousand-year-old tree and they say, what the hey. They don't respect it, you know? Thing's just growing out of the ground. But to cut to the detail, this bed comes to you from Indonesia fresh from a managed forest, what they call a managed forest, and it hasn't been treated yet so you've got to care for it. You've got to oil it at least once a year. It's like it's still alive. The molecules are still stretching and expanding. I admit it's not like a fine piece of furniture that your grandmother might have taken pride in and cared for because it isn't a fine piece of furniture, it's hacked out by simple Malay Archipelago artisans for export. With fairly crude tools. Now some people like this situation, it's just what they want. They want to feel they're doing their part by providing a commitment, a commitment to life, a thwarted life, not just to an inert tyrannical object like the kind your forebears served. And this baby's cheap. Of course the timber industry is way out of control worldwide, and this price in no way reflects the real costs entailed, the *invisible* costs you might say. But the opportunity you have right here is to acquire something that's alive even when it's dead, do you hear what I'm saying? The salesman had a head that looked like a medicine ball. How heavy that must be, Angela thought.

When it began to resemble something more like a brown dog's head, she woke up.

. . .

Darleen arrived with someone she introduced as Deke, her assistant and guide, a man older than Angela with graying, slicked-back hair. He wore a leather shirt and extremely tight-fitting leather pants which suggested no knob. Angela couldn't help but notice this. Darleen had dyed her hair white and it sprang above her pale face like a web composed of bristles and points. She had not, however, adorned her face with rings or studs, as was so much the fashion among the young. The rings always seemed to presuppose some sort of leash to Angela. She was pleased that Darleen had not succumbed to convention.

"Slippery out," the man said.

He requested upon arrival a bath. His bathing was noisy and prolonged, and when he emerged from Angela's bathroom the immediate premises smelled fruity and foul. "Bag?" he said to Darleen.

"I put it in the kitchen."

Angela heard him opening and shutting drawers, criticizing the color scheme—green and red or "rhubarb"—and bemoaning the dearth of protein. There was then the sound of a bottle being uncorked. He appeared with a single water goblet filled to the brim with wine. "Glasses look as if they were washed on the inside only," he complained. "Knives badly in need of sharpening." He stood before them, sipping the wine appreciatively. Angela's eyes reluctantly strayed to his remarkable leather pants.

"Can't see nothing for seeing something else," Deke muttered.

"Dear. . . ," Angela began.

"I want to marry him, Mummy, I'll spend years if necessary nursing him back to health. I want a large wedding in an English garden with a champagne fountain." She chewed on her fingers and laughed.

Angela decided to ignore the subject and presence of Deke, assistant and guide, for the moment. "Is everything going well at school? Tell me about school."

"We have finished our studies of archaic cultures with the Aztecs. As everywhere else in the world, the Aztec elite had more varied ideas about their gods than the common people."

"Don't you go believing that now!" Deke exclaimed.

"Religious thinking among the elite developed into a real philosophy which stressed the relative nature of all things," Darleen continued briskly. "Such a philosophy can only develop in a sophisticated environment."

She then lapsed into silence. Deke said he was going to take a peek around if it didn't disaccommodate anyone.

"What will you be doing this summer?" Angela asked after a while. "Will you be a nanny again for the Marksons?"

"I hardly think so." Darleen gazed at her critically. At some point in boarding school she had learned how to enlarge her eyes and make them glassy at will, like some carnivore about to attack.

"I was on the island just yesterday but I didn't walk as far as their house."

"Am I supposed to find that interesting?" Darleen sighed. "In another class we're reading Dante. Do you know why he called it a comedy?" She raised a gnawed paw to prevent her mother from replying, although Angela had no intention of interrupting her. "Because it progresses from a dark beginning to redemption and hope."

"What translation are you using?"

"Oh for godssakes, Binyon. Laurence Binyon. What do you care? That's not the point I wish to make. The point I wish to make is that Dante's imagination was primarily visual. In his time people didn't dream, they had visions. And these visions had meaning. We only have dreams and dreams are haphazard and undisciplined, the meager vestige of a once great method of immediate knowing." She gnawed on her fingers again. "You see visions today and you're considered abnormal, uncouth."

Deke hurried past them back into the kitchen, where he poured more wine.

"This ain't much of an establishment if you pardon my saying so," he said to Angela. "No steaks in the freezer, no ice cream, sound system inadequate, music fit only to disinform the listener, no point in hearing it twice, towels thin, washcloths worn and most suspect, bed lumpy, poor recycling practices, few spare lightbulbs on hand, fire extinguishers out of date, no playing cards, clocks not set properly—"

"I like them a little fast," Angela conceded. It was all true. He was in no way exaggerating.

"Potted violets on windowsill in very poor condition, worst case of powdery mildew I ever saw. I could go on."

"I remember those violets," Darleen said. "Those violets are from my childhood."

"Now that's just plain wrong," Angela protested.

"Suffering the same fate regardless," Darleen said.

"You got a considerable amount of canned goods, however.

Can I take some back to my friends?" Deke's hair was still wet, but already scurf was bedecking his thin shoulders like fresh snow.

"See, Mummy, even though a person has no future to speak of, he can take a moment to think of others. He can trust even in the blackest part of night that the daylight is not going to forget to come back for him."

"She's a talker, isn't she," Deke said.

"That surprises me, actually," Angela confessed. "It really does." She was brooding about that daylight-coming-back business. You couldn't think that way about daylight, that's why the ancients were always so hysterical. It was just too mental, too neurasthenic. Certain things just couldn't forget to come back. And when they finally didn't, it wasn't because they *forgot*. They did it with deliberation.

Deke had casually resumed his litany of the inadequacies of Angela's method of living. "Carpeting not particularly clean—gritty, in fact. No handy cold-care tissues available, no Proust."

"For godssakes," Darleen said, "you're the biggest show-off I've ever known for someone who a couple hours ago was begging outside the bus station."

"Selling newspapers," Deke said.

"They were giveaway papers," Darleen said. "They were supposed to be free." She turned to her mother. "I was kind of not looking forward to us being together. I needed a respite from you at first. So I gave this one fifty dollars to come here with me."

"You want it back?" From a slit pocket in his shirt he extracted a bill, then proceeded to unfold Benjamin Franklin's enormous head.

"Yes, she does," Angela said. "Of course she does." She sent Darleen a hundred dollars every month for, the word they had agreed upon was *incidentals,* and she certainly did not want her to be disposing of the money in this fashion. "I send you a hundred—"

"Big goddamn deal," Darleen said. "My roommate gets two hundred each month from her parents, which they earn by collecting cans and bottles. The Garcias search the streets and alleys thirteen hours a day for cans and bottles. It's their god-damn job. Fifteen thousand cans pay their rent each month and another six thousand nets their little scholar Isabelle two hundred bucks each month, and I am informing you that Isabelle—who's the biggest goddamn snob I've ever met—spends it on fancy underwear. The Garcias are tiny, selfless, worn-out *saints* walking the earth, I've seen 'em, and Isabelle buys *lingerie.*" She waved the proffered bill away. "What's gone is gone," she said, and laughed.

Deke refolded the bill and placed it back in his shirt. "She's probably referring to an unfortunate erotic crisis I underwent recently. Otherwise, given its more general application, I would say that she doesn't subscribe to the gone-is-gone theory one bit."

Darleen scowled at him. "This is not the appropriate moment."

Deke sniffed loudly, rotated his arms and clasped his hands together. "Cold in here too. Not cozy. Only thing of interest is this old painting. Where'd you get this? Quite out of place. An odd choice, I'd say."

It was a large oil of beavers and their home on a lake, painted the century before. It was not in a frame but affixed to the wall by nails. Angela looked at it, resting her chin in her hand thoughtfully. The colors of the landscape were deep and lustrous. The water was a fervent rumpled barren of green, the trees along the curving shore like cloaked messengers. Everything seemed fresh and clean with kind portent, even the sky. God had poured his being in equal measure to all creatures, Angela thought solemnly, to each as much as it could receive. Beavers were peculiar and reclusive, but that was their nature. They were not frivolous beings. They behaved responsibly and gravely and with great fidelity. Here they were involved in the process of constructing their house, carrying branches and twigs and so forth in their jaws and on their great paddle-like tails, though the structure was already large and in Angela's view extremely accomplished, a mansion, in fact, the floors of which were carpeted with boughs of softest evergreen, the windows curving out over the water like balconies for the enjoyment of the air.

"Mummy stole that painting," Darleen said.

"Well, good for you!" Deke said. Clearly, Angela had been elevated in his regard.

"Some years ago, Mummy used to be quite the drinker," Darleen said.

"Is that so!" Deke exclaimed, more delighted still. "Why'd you give it up?"

The painting had been in a roadhouse she once frequented. Sitting and drinking, pretty much alone in that unpopular place, she would watch the painting with all her heart. Slowly her heavy heart would turn light and she would feel it pulling away as though it wasn't responsible for her anymore, freeing her to slip beneath the glittering skein of water into the lovely clear beaver world of woven light where everything was wild and orderly and real. A radiant inhuman world of speechless grace. This was where she spent her time when she could. These were delicate moments, however, and further weak cocktails never prolonged them. Further cocktails, actually, no matter how responsibly weak, only propelled her to the infelicitous surface again. The artist, the bastard, had probably trapped and drowned the beavers and thrust rods through their poor bodies to arrange them in life-assuming positions, as Audubon had done with birds, the bastard, and Stubbs had done with horses, the bastard, to make his handsome portraits.

"Your mother isn't very forthcoming with the details, is she?" Deke said.

"I would wake up weeping," Angela said. "Tears would be streaming down my face."

"You quit, and now they don't anymore?" Deke asked suspiciously.

Angela stared at him.

"Doesn't seem much to give up the drink for, a few tears. How long's it been since you've cried now?"

"Oh, years," Angela said.

"And now her heart's a little ice-filled crack. Isn't it, Mummy?" Darleen said.

"Why don't you leave your mother alone for a while," Deke said. "Look at you. You're a vicious little being, like one of those thylacines."

"The Tasmanian wolf is extinct," Darleen said. "Don't show off so goddamn much."

"Their prey was sheeps," Deke said. "But the sheeps won out in the end. They always do."

"Sheeps," Darleen snickered.

"A vicious little being you are," Deke repeated mildly. He regarded the painting once more. "I got a friend knew a guy who lived with a beaver in the Adirondacks. Every time my friend would go visit him, that beaver would be there with its own big beaver house made of sticks and such right in this guy's cabin. He'd rescued this beaver and they had a really good relationship. You broke bread with my friend's friend and you'd break bread with that beaver."

"Mummy, when do you plan on serving supper?" Darleen said. "She never has food in this house," she said to Deke.

"She's got a number of vegetables ready to go. Vegetables are good for you," he said without much conviction.

At dinner, Angela felt impelled to ask him how he and Darleen had met and what, exactly, it was that he did.

"This is what I got to say to that remark. I don't know if you read much, but there's a story by Anton Chekhov called 'Gooseberries.' And in this story one of the characters says in conversation that there should be a man with a hammer reminding every happy, contented individual that they're not going to be happy forever. This man with a hammer should be banging on the door of the happy individual's house or something to that effect."

"You think you're the man with the hammer?"

Deke smiled at her modestly.

"If I recall that story correctly," Angela said, "the point being made about the man with the hammer is that there is no such person." Angela had attended boarding school herself. She remembered almost everything she had been alerted to then and very little afterwards.

"You're so negative, Mummy. You dispute anything anyone has to say," Darleen crouched over the table with her fist wrapped around a fork, not eating.

"The man with the hammer that I recall is in another story, not by Chekhov at all. In *A Mother's Tale* the circumstances couldn't be more . . ."

"Don't be tiresome, Mummy," Darleen said.

"Why don't you leave your mother alone, the poor woman," Deke said. "This is an ordinary woman here. Where's the challenge? Why do you hate her so much? Your hate's misplaced, I'd say."

"Why do I hate Mummy?"

"Not at all clear. Whoa, though, whoa, I got a question for Angela. You ever confess under questioning from this child that you had considered, if only for an instant when she was but the size of a thumb inside you, not having this particular one at all, maybe a later one?"

"No," Angela said.

Deke nodded. "That's nice," he said. He picked at his potato. "This is a little overcooked," he said.

"I just want to check on something," Darleen said. She disappeared into what had been her bedroom. There was the ugly wallpaper in a dense tweedy pattern which would make anyone feel as though they were trapped under a basket. Darleen had selected it at the age of eight. Angela didn't use the room for storage. Technically, it was still Darleen's bedroom.

"Dinner was OK, actually OK," Deke said pleasantly. "Glad you didn't go the fowl route. You ever had goose? There's this wealthy woman in town and she's got this perturberance about nuisance geese. They're Canada geese but they're not from Canada, she says, and she's got the town to agree to capture and slaughter them and feed them to the poor. If you have any influence, would you tell that old girl we don't like those geese? The flavor is off. They're golf course geese and full of insecticides and effluent and such."

"Betty Bishop!" Angela exclaimed. "Why, I just broke her wrist!"

"Good for . . ." Deke began, then stopped.

"It was an accident, but what a coincidence!"

"I guess you wouldn't have the influence I seek then," Deke said, sniffing. "You ever get the air ducts in this place cleaned? Should be cleaned annually. Dust, fungi, bacteria—you're cohabiting with continually recirculating pollutants here."

Darleen returned. "Where's my little fish," she demanded.

"Well, it, oh goodness, it's been years," Angela said.

"Is that my fish's bowl in the kitchen filled with pennies and shit?"

"I saw that," Deke said. "Clearly a fishbowl, now much reduced in circumstances."

"I had a little fish throughout my childhood," Darleen explained to him. "I said 'Good morning' to it in the morning and 'Good night' to it at night."

Deke stretched out his long, black-wrapped legs.

"For years and years I had this little fish," Darleen said. "But it wasn't the same fish! I'd pretend I hadn't noticed there was something awfully wrong with fishie sometimes before I went to school, and she would pretend she hadn't slipped the deceased down the drain and run out and bought another one before my return."

"Oh, I knew you knew," Angela said.

"If it had been the same fish, you two would have lacked the means to communicate with each other at all," Deke suggested.

"Mummy, I want to be serious now. Do you know why I'm here? I'm here because Daddy Bruce requested that I come. That's why I'm here."

For an instant, Angela had no idea who Daddy Bruce was. Then her heart pitched about quite wildly. Darleen had neglected to put her eyes in full deployment and she gazed at her mother with alarming sincerity.

"I was studying one night. I'd been up for hours and hours. It was very late and he just appeared, in my mind, not corporeally, and he said, 'Honey, this is Daddy Bruce. I don't want you cutting yourself off from your mom and me anymore. Your mom's a painful thing to apprehend but you've got to try. She's living her life like a clock does, just counting the hours. You can take a clock from room to room, from place to place, but all it does is count the hours.'"

"He never talked that way!" Angela exclaimed. "He was just a boy!"

"Well, that's what happens pretty quick," Deke said. "They all get to sounding the same. It's characteristic of death's drear uniformity. Most difficult to be pluralistic when you're dead."

"He said he never loved you and he's sorry about that now."

Angela's heart was pounding hard and insistently, distracting her a little, making a great obtrusive show of itself. Be aware of me, it was pounding, be aware.

"He said if he had to do it all over, he still wouldn't love you but you wouldn't know it."

"It don't seem as if this Bruce is giving Angela much of a second chance here," Deke said.

"Daddy Bruce wanted to assure you that—"

"Tell him not to worry about it," Angela said. There were worse things, she supposed, than being told you had never been loved by a dead man.

Deke giggled. "What else he have to say? Did he suggest you were studying too hard?"

"He would hardly have bothered to come all the way from the other world to tell me that," Darleen said.

"I suspect there's only one thing to know about that other world," Deke opined. "You don't go to it when you're dead. That other world exists only when you're in this one."

"Yes, that's right," Angela said. She took a deep uncertain breath.

"That might be correct," Darleen said, gnawing on her hands again. "The dead are part of our community, just like those in prison."

"Ever visit the prison gift shop?" Deke said. "Can't be more than ten miles from here. They sell cutting boards, boot scrapers, consoles for entertainment centers. The ladies knit those toilet-seat covers, toaster covers. Nice things. Reasonable. They won't let the ones on death row contribute anything, though. They want to sell products, not freak collector items. It's like that tree used to be outside the First Congregational Church. That big old copper beech they cut down because they said it was a suicide magnet? Wouldn't use the wood for nothing either, and that was good wood. Threw it in the landfill. Tree was implicated in only four deaths. Drew in two unhappy couples was all. Wouldn't think they'd rip out a three-hundred-year-old tree for that, but down it went. And now they've got a little sapling there no bigger around than a baseball bat."

Angela dismayed herself by laughing.

"That's right," Deke giggled. "If a young person gets it in his mind now passing that spot, he's got to *wait*."

"I should have suspected you two would get along," Darleen said sourly.

"You sick?" Deke asked Angela. "Is that why you don't care so much? Some undiagnosed cancer?"

"She's never been sick a day in her life," Darleen said. "She has the constitution of a horse."

"Horses are actually quite delicate," Deke said. "Lots can go wrong with a horse, naturally, and then you can make additional things go wrong, should you wish, if it's in your interests."

"Deke worked a few summers in Saratoga," Darleen said. She suddenly looked weary.

"A sick horse is a dead horse, pretty much," Deke said. "I'm going to uncork that other bottle now." From the kitchen, Angela heard him excoriating the rust on the gas jets, the lime buildup around the sink fixtures, the poorly applied adhesive plastic covering meant to suggest crazed Italian tiles. Goblet once again brimming, he did not resume his place at the table but walked over to the painting. "I can see why you felt you had to have this," he said. "At first it appears to be realistically coherent and pleasantly decorative, but the viewer shortly becomes aware of a sense of melancholy, of disturbing presentiment."

Angela wondered if it was possible to desire a drink any more than she did at this moment. It couldn't be.

"You clearly got an affinity with unknowing, unprepared creatures," Deke went on.

"Deke used to be an art critic," Darleen said.

He waved one hand dismissively. "Just for the prison newsletter."

"Yeah, Deke attended prison for two years," Darleen said.

"I began my thesis there," Deke said. "'Others: Do They Exist?' But I never completed it. I was a couple of hundred pages into it when I had to admit to myself that it wasn't genuine breakthrough thinking."

Angela rose to her feet suddenly and tried to embrace Darleen. The girl was all stubborn bone. Her clothes smelled musty, and a stinging chemical odor rose from her spiky hair. She pulled away easily from Angela's grasp.

"Whoa, whoa, whoa there," Deke said.

Darleen laughed. "Daddy Bruce better get here quick. Wake you up."

"I have to . . . I have to . . ."

They looked at her.

"It's late and I have to go to work tomorrow," she said, ashamed.

"You said you'd take the day off!" Darleen cried.

"Take the day off, it don't fit when you put it on again," Deke said. "Attention here, I'm taking the fishbowl and going out for more wine. Liquor store has one of those change machines. Those things are fun, you ever seen one work?"

"Don't leave!" Angela and Darleen exclaimed together.

"At a dangerously low level," he said, raising the bottle.

No one could argue that it was otherwise.

"Just stay a little while longer," Darleen pleaded.

Deke pursed his lips and pressed his hands to his leather shirt. "I might commence to pace," he said. He grimly poured out the last of the wine.

"There was a strange thing that happened last night,"

Angela began. "I was on a boat, the boat that goes to the islands. I wasn't actually there, but the most remarkable coincidence—"

"A coincidence is something that's going to happen and does," Deke said. "You got a fondness for the word, I notice."

"Oh, Mummy is so seldom precise," Darleen said. "When I was small, she would tell me I had my father's eyes. Then one day I finally said, 'I do not have his eyes. He was not an organ donor to my knowledge. A little frigging precision in language would be welcome,' I said."

Deke looked at her impatiently, then stood as though yanked up by a rope. "You girls hold off on the Daddy Bruce business until I get back. That's dangerous business. You don't want to go too far with that without an impartial yet expert observer present."

He left without further farewell bearing the fishbowl, the door shutting softly behind him.

Angela laughed. "I think we disappointed him."

The room felt stifling. She opened a window, beyond which was a storm window, a so-called combination window, adaptable to the seasons. She fumbled with the aluminum catches and pushed it up. The cold clutched her, then darted past. She turned and looked at her daughter. "I love you," she said.

"Mummy, Mummy," Darleen sighed. Then, tolerantly, "The new headmaster has a white umbrella cockatoo that likes to be rocked like a baby."

"Do tell me about it, please," Angela said.

"Stupid bird," Darleen said cheerfully.

· · ·

Six years later, Angela was dying in the town's hospital, in a room where many before her had passed. She had known none of them, but this room they had in common, and the old business engaged in there. Darleen had been summoned but would not arrive in time. Angela was fifty years old. She had not gotten out as early as she might have certainly, but now by chance she had firmly grasped death's tether.

Passed that little sapling tree on the way here, Deke said. Still being permitted to grow in the churchyard. Too new yet to cast a shadow, but it had better mind its manners, no?

Angela wanted to laugh, even now. What a night that had been!

Most enjoyable evening, Deke agreed.

The first nurse said, "It sounded like, 'Did you bring the hammer?'"

The other nurse said, "Sometimes their voices can be remarkably clear. You can really understand them. I had one say, 'I don't want to go back there.' Just as clear as could be."

The first nurse did not like this one. She was new and ambitious, quite often imprudent. "Are you sure?" she demanded.

FORTUNE

IT WAS THE PARENTS! When would the parents stop coming? They'd been coming for months, since Christmas, since *before* Christmas, since the burning of the Devil festivities on the seventh. June's mother and her second husband had arrived, missing Howard's parents by only a few days, for they had come down specifically for his twenty-second birthday. Caroline's father had come down for Valentine's Day with his new wife and their fairly new infant to show her to Caroline, as though she cared. Abby's parents were still in town, having arrived for Semana Santa—Holy Week, which was now just past—and James's parents would be showing up any day now from Roatón, off Honduras, where they had been diving. And each set of parents had a new child with them. There was Emily and Morgan and Parker and Bailey and Henry, not one of them over the age of six. It was a phenomenon.

The parents were generous when they visited. June's mother's new husband chartered a plane and flew them all to

Tikal. They climbed Pyramid IV and watched the sunrise, even baby Morgan in her tiny safari ensemble. And even though June's mother's new husband had rented rooms for them at the Jungle Lodge, one night they'd slept out among the ruins in hammocks. Everyone knew this was the desired, anecdotal thing to do, sleeping out among the ruins beneath the bats during a full moon, which it happened to be that night. Then they flew back to Antigua for the parade of the heads, for this is what they had really come for, to see the huge papier-mâché heads, the *gigantes* and *cabezudos*, running and weaving down the streets beneath the fireworks and whistling rockets. June's mother and her new husband had expensive cameras and they took pictures of everything, they were delighted with everything.

When Howard's parents came, the father, a prominent throat specialist, rented horses for everyone and they had ridden to one of the lakes for a picnic. Even baby Bailey made the trip, wrapped in his mother's arms with one tiny hand clinging to the pommel. The whole group of them, eight in all, trotting like a cavalry through the poor little towns on these big-assed horses, leaving behind piles of green-flecked dung. Where had they gotten such healthy horses? It was embarrassing. *Buenos días!* Howard's parents said to anything that moved. It was amazing they hadn't been stoned.

Caroline's father appeared with darling Emily, a redhead, and his lively new redheaded wife, who wore a ring in her navel and was only two years older than Caroline. There had actually been something of an incident when everyone had been invited for lunch in the garden of the Hotel Antigua. There were some hummingbirds in the hibiscus bush near them, green and purple ones, the size of mice. One veered toward

Emily in her high chair, no doubt encouraged by the feathery brilliance of her hair, and her attentive mother smacked it sharply with a guidebook she was holding. The bird spun to the ground in a buzzing heap.

They all shrank back from it a little.

"Gee, Penny," Caroline said.

"It was coming right at the baby," Penny said. "It almost struck her."

"Hummers can be exceptionally aggressive," Howard said, smirking.

"Maybe it's just stunned," June said. "Maybe if we put it under a bush."

James took a linen napkin from the table and placed it over the bird, which was still whirring like a windup toy. Darling Emily bounced in the high chair and clapped her hands. She wore a sweet little dress embroidered with ducks. James walked a ways beyond the table and was about to lay the humming-bird down.

"Farther," June said. "A farther bush."

He came back with the napkin and put it on the table.

"James," Abby said, "is that blood?"

He picked it up again and refolded it.

"Maybe we should have eaten it," Howard said. "You know, so as not to waste it. We should find its nest and eat that too. The Chinese eat nests."

Penny frowned at him. "I *am* sorry," she said. She dabbed at the plate of fruit she had been feeding Emily. "What is this, guava? Or papaya? One of them upsets her tummy."

Another pitcher of margaritas appeared from somewhere. It was a very well-run place. Gardeners swept the walks quietly with palm fronds tied to sticks. One of the swimming pools had the heads of a hundred ivory-colored roses floating in the deep end.

"You're great kids," Caroline's father said. "Really, you're terrific kids." Clearly, his spirits had taken more of a beating from the hummingbird incident than his wife's. "You're fine kids. Caroline, you have fine friends," he said.

All the visiting parents liked to pretend that the young people were charming. It was funny seeing this, all of them pretending this in their own way. The children were exhausted by the parents' vigor, they felt wearied by their presence. They were repelled by the parents' dedicated interest in them, they were astonished. Will we ever be *this* blind, do you think? they'd say. No, they agreed, they could not imagine themselves being this blind . . .

They were all starting off in their twenties. Each had come separately to this colonial town in the bowl-shaped valley beneath the three volcanoes and found one another here. Each of them remembered their first solitary days in town and then the speed with which they became involved in a life with the others, their friends. And they still wondered how this had been accomplished, and how much of it they had each been responsible for. They felt that here their lives were now beginning.

At the same time, they felt it was possible that their actual lives were still waiting for them, and that it involved different people. This was something they found themselves thinking about more and more, usually with unhappiness, as the parents kept coming.

Holy Week and its enormous, numbing spectacle was over for another year. The great obligation was over. The great *anda* borne by the penitents had been stored. The dyed sawdust and fresh flowers that had covered the streets in elaborate designs before being mangled by the penitents' feet had been swept away. Everyone loved Good Friday—betrayal and trial and cruelty still having the power to captivate—but Easter was a letdown. The promise of Easter was the same old promise. The town was hot and quiet, and everyone was still a little drunk.

Abby and June were having breakfast at one of the cafes that faced the park. The fountain was not operative this morning. Usually water plashed from the stone nipples of a trio of heroically sculpted women, but today they stood inactive, though still with their mysteriously withdrawn expressions as they held their lovely breasts. Workmen in boots rooted around in the water beneath them.

"I think your parents are cute," June said. "They're not like Howard's. Poor Howard."

"I spent ten to two with them yesterday," Abby said. "Then I took them to the market and my mother would say about anything, 'Is this the best price you can give me? Is this the best you can do?' In English, of course, slowly, in English. Candles, bananas, those tiny bags of confetti, everything . . . She bought me lightbulbs, she insisted. 'You have all these dead lightbulbs,' she said, and I said, 'Mom, we can buy these in the store, we don't have to be bargaining for them in the market.' Then I had to spend six to nine with them too, back at the hotel. And that Parker! He had to run across the cobblestones, and of course he falls down and practically tears off his kneecap. Finally, I cracked. I said, 'I've got to have a day off. I can't have another meal with you for a while, I just can't,' and my father said, 'We aren't taking out taxes.'"

191

June laughed, but then she said, "What did he mean?"

"Maybe he said withholding," Abby said. "It was a joke. Like I thought it was a job, my being with them."

"Oh, that's funny," June said. "That's what I mean. They're not that bad."

"I can't believe they adopted that child and then named him Parker," Abby said. "Where did that name come from? My mother reminded me that I had promised to take him tonight so they could go out to dinner by themselves."

"When my mother was here and I was with her at the bank?" June said earnestly. "And I was sitting there looking at my mother in line to get money? I had an epiphany."

"Really," Abby said.

"It was . . . my mother will always love me."

"That's an epiphany?" Abby said.

"It wasn't a thought. It was like . . ." June trailed off. "Your mother will always love you too, forever, no matter what."

"Isn't that amazing," Abby said. "Really, it's amazing, if it's true."

A young Guatemalan boy wearing filthy green shorts with a broken zipper and a Chicago Bulls T-shirt came into the cafe holding three glass Shangri-La bottles by the neck. Then they saw Caroline walking by with her brown long-legged dog on a rope leash.

"Caroline!" they cried together.

She joined them, dragging the dog in with her. He had been neutered not long before, and he had a plastic basket on his head so he wouldn't rip his stitches out. The stitches should have been taken out by now and the basket removed, but Caroline was putting it off even though the Indians laughed rudely at the sight of them. Neither Abby nor June would have been capable of walking a dog around town with a basket on its head.

"Can't we take that off the poor thing?" Abby said.

"I know, I know, but then he bites his fleas," Caroline said. "I've got to give him a bath first."

The dog smacked the basket against the table leg and lay down with a thump. He was an odd little dog with large dewclaws and a strangely malformed mouth. Caroline had bought him in the market for two quetzales, about thirty-five cents. She took excellent care of him in a somewhat unbalanced way and was always trying to improve him. Caroline was an artist, she had always been an artist, things just came to her sometimes. She was thin, almost ascetic-looking, and had a temper.

Abby continued to look at the dog, at its long fawn-colored legs that seemed so breakable. Pets made Abby feel discouraged. In the run-down motel where they all rented rooms by the month, the guardian had an aged, arthritic parrot who was brought out on a stick every morning and left to hobble around on a broken bench beneath some banana trees until dusk. Sometimes June would gently spray him with water from the hose, which seemed to neither distress nor delight him, Abby didn't know why she bothered. The motel also housed some members of a street band, who were seldom there, and a morose man with a bulging vein in his forehead which appeared to beat incessantly. He made a living from his fortune birds—three yellow canaries in a bamboo cage that would tell your future by selecting a small rolled piece of paper from a pinewood box. The tiny prophets' names were Profeta, Planeta and Justicio, and they seemed happy and untroubled. The motel was not far from the *parque central* and was next to one of the town's many ruined cathedrals, the rubble from one of the cathedral's walls making up part of the courtyard. The rooms were small, dark and cold, but each had a perfect view of Agua, the most beautiful of the volcanoes.

The Guatemalan child, having been paid for the bottles, was threading his way back through the tables. He paused and gazed beseechingly at June's pancake, which she had barely touched. Abby had not eaten hers either and was using the plate more or less as an ashtray.

"June," Caroline said.

June looked at the boy. "Sure, sure," she said. He plucked up the pancake with slender fingers and hurried outside. He crossed the street and stared at June as he ate.

"Is he scowling at us?" June said. "I mean, what is it exactly one is supposed to do?"

The others would often tease June for being so grave about everything. She wore oversized American clothes, a plaid shirt and brown shorts, and a woven necklace that her mother had bought her during her visit. June had wanted the necklace badly and had led her mother to the store, which was frequently closed, more than once. She affected ragged black and blond hair which she made sticky with shaving cream.

"Imagine him and Parker as playmates," Caroline said. "Little playmates."

"That is so radical," Abby said.

The boy finished the pancake, then turned modestly away from them to urinate.

"Oh, gaaa," June said.

"My mother is finally beginning to notice the public urination," Abby said. "'You know, honey,' she said, 'this is a lovely town, but so much public urination goes on. I don't think I've ever seen so much public urination. You walk through the park and men are urinating behind pieces of cardboard. Boys are urinating on flowers. We went to look at some churches and we were picking our way around the courtyard and an old man was urinating on a pile of sand. When he finished he flapped his hands at us. He scolded us! He said we were not supposed to be in the courtyard, we could only be in the church. He was the ostiary or something, or thought he was . . .'" Abby was mimicking her mother's nasal, bemused way of speaking.

"They're still here, your parents?" Caroline said.

"Oh god, yes," Abby said. "I have to watch Parker tonight so they can go out. It's their anniversary."

"We'll all watch him," Caroline said. "We'll sit around in a circle and blow smoke at him or something. Howard will ask him his opinion of death."

"That is getting so old," Abby said. "It's like an old bar trick or something."

"Morgan's been the darlingest," Caroline said to June. "Don't you just love her?"

June blushed. "Do you know what my mother told me?" June said. "She told me she had always been emotionally indifferent to my father, from the very first, but now she had found happiness and she hoped that I would find such happiness and never have to spend long years with someone I was emotionally indifferent to."

"Oh," Caroline said. "It's like a little blessing she gave you, isn't it? That's so nice."

"I love watching June blush," Abby said. "Really, June, you are so funny."

Then she and Caroline talked about how they wished they

had a car they could share. Then they began talking about how James claimed to have stolen a car in Texas and driven it through Mexico into Guatemala, where he'd sold it for a great deal of money in the capital. This was a difficult, virtually impossible feat and the story had always elicited considerable admiration. James also claimed that once, prior to stealing the car, he had been arrested in California for underage drinking, and that as part of his sentencing he was forced to attend the autopsy of a drunk driver. He described the way they had sawed off the top of the dead man's head and lifted it like "a lid on a basket."

"I think he made up that stuff about the cadaver," Abby said.

"I didn't believe that for one minute," Caroline said.

"I don't know about that car from Texas either," Abby said. "He's so enthusiastic about that experience, he probably didn't have it."

"What are you thinking, June?" Abby asked.

"I was thinking I have no sense of direction," June said. "I can't remember the names of flowers or ruins or saints. And I can't keep a journal. Any journal I keep sucks." She was thinking of Edith Holden's precious Edwardian journal with all the lovely drawings. The one she had in prep school. Edith Holden had died tragically young, drowning in the Thames while collecting horse chestnut buds, the twit.

The bill arrived and June began to go over it painstakingly. "Excuse me, pardon me. *Perdóneme?*" she called to the waitress, "but no one here ordered the *huevos revueltos.*"

"Oh, just pay for it," Abby said. "All that stuff is fifty cents or something, isn't it? I'll pay for it."

"No, it's my turn," June said, counting out some coins.

They then got up with a great scraping of chairs on the ugly tiles.

On the street, the dog strained toward a mound of burnt plastic in the gutter and managed to acquire something repellent before Caroline hauled him away.

"He is so dim," she said. "I thought fixing him would make him smarter."

"That is so funny," Abby said.

They reached the heavy scarred wooden doors of their compound. They pushed them open and Caroline unknotted the rope from the dog's collar. He leapt into the air and ran around the courtyard three times at remarkable speed before a bougainvillea stump snagged the basket and sent him sprawling. The parrot dropped the piece of mango he'd been toying with and crouched against the gnawed slats of his bench. The parrot's name was Nevertheless as far as anyone could translate it. The dog didn't have a name.

The fortune birds were not up yet. Customarily they rested until noon in their cage, beneath a clean dish towel. For them Easter week was one of the biggest weeks of the year. They had told a thousand fortunes. Their director, the man with the staggeringly large vein, was sitting at a card table in a corner of the courtyard writing new fortunes in an elegant script on blue pieces of paper. He wrote swiftly, without reflection or emotion. James and Howard were playing Hacky Sack on the grass with a tiny stitched ball that said *I ♥ Jesus* on it. They had bought it from some evangelicals who did massage. The boys had been so dumped the night before, clutching their glasses of *aguardiente,* that they could hardly find their mouths. Now here they were, sleek and quick.

June blushed when she saw James, for she had drunk a

great deal of *aguardiente* last night as well and recalled asking him, "Do you think I have a personality?"

"No," he had said.

"A personality," she persisted.

"Why would you want one? You're fine."

"But I should," June said.

"Look at my wallet," he said. It was a long leather wallet clipped by a chain to his belt. "There was a whole bin of these at the airport on sale and the merchant said that each wallet had its own personality because it was natural material and the lines and colors and imperfections made each one unique."

"That's sick," June had said.

"Personality is secondary to predicament," James had said.

She was attracted to James, to his deep-set eyes and perfect skin, but none of them were lovers. That would have spoiled everything. Love was a compromise, they felt. They were not like their parents, who were always in love and who just went on and on with life, changing partners, acquiring new children, abandoning past interests and assuming new ones, always in love with someone or something.

It was almost noon. The boys continued to play Hacky Sack, thrusting out their long feet.

"I'm going to wash the dog," Caroline announced. "After which we shall remove the basket." She produced some special soap she had bought at the market. It came in a small box that had the drawing of an insect on it.

"It doesn't really look like a flea, though," Abby noted.

"They intended it to look like a flea," Caroline said confidently.

They captured the dog and poured a bucket of water over

his wiry coat. The soap made a quick brown lather and almost instantly, motionless black fleas appeared.

"Look at those fleas," Abby said. "They're enormous."

"This soap must be lethal," June said.

The guardian and his family came out to watch the dog being bathed. The parrot watched, too, swaying excitedly. The dog stood passively, his head bent, the basket touching the ground.

They rinsed and scrubbed, then rinsed again. There were fewer fleas at the end but there were never no fleas at all.

"Shouldn't we have gloves?" June asked.

"The fortune dog," Caroline said. "Divination by fleas." She picked them off. "This is not good," she said. "This is not good. This is not good either."

Then there was the ceremony of removing the basket, which was attached to the dog's collar with thick, dirty tape. Finally the basket was wrenched off. The dog's head looked somewhat smaller than anyone remembered.

"He really is unsatisfactory, isn't he?" Caroline said. "Maybe if I straightened his tail. He needs something. What do you think, June?"

"Maybe a bandanna," June said.

"Oh, I hate bandannas on dogs," Caroline said. "The vet said he had too many teeth in his mouth. A couple of them should be pulled. And see all those warts on his head? They keep growing back."

The dog squatted on his haunches and stared at them. He had probably never been meant for this life. He was just not consubstantial with this life.

One of the reasons Caroline had acquired the dog was to

practice concern. They all felt that sometimes it was necessary to practice the more subtle emotions.

The dog suddenly widened his eyes as though in delighted recall, shot up and sideways and danced away to his favorite spot in the compound, the smoldering refuse pile in one of the stalls that once stabled horses, rooting about for only an instant before finding something ragged and foul which he settled down to eat. At the same time, the owner of the fortune birds capped his pen, rose from his chair, rolled his shoulders, crouched slightly to fart and removed the cloth from the little birds' cage. Immediately the birds began to sing.

It was a lovely day. White clouds streamed past Agua, but low, so that its dark cone was visible against the bright blue sky.

"I want to do something today," Abby said. "Don't you?"

From a distance Agua was magnificent, but they had all climbed it once and found it disappointing.

Abby looked at her watch. She said, "If I got this wet, I'd die."

"Let's climb Fuego," Howard said, giving the Hacky Sack a final, unraveling kick.

"It's too late," Abby said. "We'd have to start earlier than this." Fuego, the live volcano, was no higher than Agua but the ascent was more difficult. The third volcano, Acatenango, commanded little interest though surely it had its dignity, its dangers and charms.

"Never too late to climb Fuego," James said. "The hot one, the mean one."

"Oh, that damn Fuego," Caroline said.

They had never climbed it, although they had set out to do so more than once. They would stay up all night and dawn would bring with it the desire to climb Fuego. They would take a taxi to Alotenango, a poor town surrounded by dark coffee trees, from which the ascent began. They would climb for a while, floundering through the greasy ash. Rocky furrows ran alongside the trail like empty rivers and sometimes became the trail. The furrow would deepen and vanish and a faint path through the ash would begin again above them. Some paths were marked by rocks painted *No!* for though these paths looked reasonable they were not at all reasonable. The rocks bore the name of a hiking club, the members of which they had never seen. They'd never seen anyone climbing, although once they saw a dead colt with a braided mane.

They had always turned back after a few hours, because what was the point really of climbing Fuego.

"I think nature's kind of senseless, actually," Caroline said. "I mean real nature. I don't get it."

The hours passed. It was midafternoon when the cage holding the fortune birds was strapped to the motorbike for the trip to the plaza.

"We should do those birds sometime," Abby said. "I can't believe they're right here with us and we've never had them tell our fortune."

"I'd want Planeta to tell mine," June said. "The one with the black eyes."

"They all have black eyes," Caroline said.

"I mean black rings around the eyes," June said.

"This earth is my home for life," James said. "Do you ever think that?"

"That is unacceptable," Howard said.

"I don't think Profeta looks that well," Caroline said. "She doesn't look as yellow. Her beak looks like it's peeling."

Caroline's dog had danced over to the motorcycle and was nosing the cage.

"Get that cur away from here or I'll break its goddamn back," the man with the remarkable vein said in startlingly clear English. The birds chirped on, hopping about in their tiny, airy rooms, the bars of which were woven with pale, wilted flowers, the floors of which were covered with the shredded faces of movie stars from shiny magazines.

Caroline hurried over and hauled the dog away. No one remarked on the outburst, recalling that it had happened before.

Shortly after the birds' departure on the black motorbike, Abby's parents arrived at the gate with young Parker and two string bags filled with food.

"Oh, I can't believe it," Abby murmured to Caroline. "So soon?"

"I'm sorry we're early," Abby's mother said, "but we went on a ruin run. We managed eight ruins today, which must be some sort of record, and when we got back to the room we discovered that we'd been robbed. Isn't that something!"

The three of them, even Parker, seemed almost enchanted that they'd been robbed, as if this were just another aspect of an exciting life. "They took nothing of real value," Abby's mother said. And that, too, added to the enjoyment of it all.

There was a little something on the side of Abby's mother's nose that perhaps had been in her nose and somehow gotten out and around onto the side of it. All of them looked at it politely. With a small adjustment in her gaze, June looked at Parker and the large white bandage he wore insouciantly on one knee. She narrowed her eyes and the child receded into some blurry future, permitting the present to be inhabited by herself and her friends, which was proper.

Abby's mother set down the bags. "There's all kinds of stuff in here," she said. "I thought you could have a picnic supper."

"That is so sweet!" Caroline said.

"What did they take?" Abby asked.

"It was so stupid of me," her mother said. "I have so much trouble locking that door. I think it's locked but it's just stuck, so the room wasn't even locked. They took this jade necklace I'd just bought. It was still wrapped in tissue. It wasn't that expensive, but the thing was I'd bought it for you. Then I thought I'd keep it, because I didn't think it was really you, and then it was stolen. It serves me right, doesn't it?"

"That's really ironic, Mom," Abby said.

June asked Abby's mother which of the ruins had been her favorite.

"I loved the convent Las Capuchinas," Abby's mother said.

"Oh, I love Las Capuchinas too!" June exclaimed, as though everyone didn't say their favorite ruin was Las Capuchinas.

"What do you think actually went on there, on that subfloor?" Abby's mother wondered. "I have three guidebooks and they all suggest something different. It was either a pantry, or for laundry, or for torture."

"You have four guidebooks," Abby's father said.

"I think it's all a matter of wild conjecture." Abby's mother raised her hand and brushed the inconsequential thing off her face. "There were twenty-five nuns, right? Twenty-four? And they were never allowed to leave except when there was an earthquake."

"I like those creepy mannequins at prayer in their cells," Caroline said.

"Don't you just want to know everything?" Abby's mother exclaimed suddenly. "Just think of all the information children Parker's age will have access to, and so quickly!"

"What's your favorite ruin?" June asked Abby's father.

"I don't have one," he said. "My favorite meal was the steak at Las Antorchas."

"I can't believe we're going back to Las Antorchas," Abby's mother said. "Honey," she said to Abby, "I'm sorry we're so early but we'll be back early. I just want to get this anniversary dinner over with."

"I don't want to stay here," Parker announced. "I want to stay with you." His hair was firmly combed. He wore madras shorts and a short-sleeved button-down shirt, dressed in a manner that small children often are for an event they are not really going to attend.

"Parker, look at that parrot!" Abby's mother said.

He studied the parrot, which was staggering across the grass to retrieve a bit of melon. "I don't like it, there's something wrong with it," he said. "I don't like that dog, either." The dog had been straining toward them soundlessly on its rope all the while, panting wildly.

"Well, just stay away from the dog," Abby's mother said. "Play with your trucks." She whispered to Abby, "We're just going to slip away now." They left and Parker sat down on the grass, dropping his head rather dramatically into his hands.

Howard went into his room and brought out an almost full bottle of Jägermeister. There was still the possibility, which they all embraced, that the liquor was made with opium. This had not been utterly discounted. "Hey, Parker," he said. "Would you like a drink?"

Parker raised his head. "I like iced tea," he said. "The kind you get at home, at the store, in a bottle. My favorite is Best Health's All Natural Gourmet Iced Tea with Lemon, and you wouldn't have that in a million years."

"He's into iced teas," Caroline said. "Isn't that scandalous."

"There's one that tastes kind of like fish," Parker said. "Sort of like rusty fish. But not right away. Just a little afterwards."

"They actually make an iced tea like that?" Howard said. "Cool."

"That is so radical," Abby said.

They drank the Jägermeister, ignoring Parker. The mosquitoes arrived. The parrot was coaxed onto a broom handle by the guardian's wife and taken in. Howard lit the paper trash and scraps of wood in the fire pit, a short, shallow trench he tended every evening. He was a big, meticulous young man. Each day he would set off with a burlap bag and scavenge for his fire pit. He kept the fire calm, he was very particular about it.

"What are you thinking, June?" James asked.

"Do the Chinese really eat nests?" she said.

"Just those of a certain bird, a kind of swift," Howard said. "The swift builds the nests out of its own saliva and the stuff hardens."

"You're kidding!" Caroline said. "Those damn Chinese."

June blushed.

"Oh, what are you thinking *now*, June?" Abby said. "You're so funny."

June had had a dream where a boy was kissing her by spitting in her mouth. He just didn't *know,* she thought. It was awful, but in the dream she was unalarmed as though this was the way it had to be done. "I was thinking about picnics. Didn't you used to have the best picnics when you were little?"

"You're too nostalgic, June," Caroline said. "Nostalgia nauseates me. I lack the nostalgic gene, thank god."

"Why do you ask her what she's thinking," Parker demanded.

"Why, because it's a game," James said. "Because she'll tell us and nobody else ever does."

"I wouldn't tell my thoughts," Parker said. "They're mine."

"But you don't have any thoughts," James said. "You're too little."

"I do too," Parker said. He was angry. He had broken one of his trucks. It was not by accident that he'd broken it, but even so.

"Well, what's one of them?" James said.

After a moment Parker said, "I like ants."

"Ants! Ants are great," Howard said. "Ants live for a long time. I read about this guy, this ant specialist who kept this queen ant and watched her for twenty-nine years. She laid eggs until she died."

"Eggs?" Parker said.

"Occasionally she allowed herself the luxury of eating one of them," Howard said. "This guy just watched his ant. What do you think? You want to do stuff like that?"

The sky was full of stars and they were beneath them, contained as if in a well.

"I'm sleepy," Parker said.

"We should have the picnic," June said. "What about the picnic?"

"What's it feel like to be adopted, Parker?" Howard asked. "You can hear me way over there, can't you?" He sprinkled out the last of the Jägermeister into their glasses. The bottle's arcane label had a stag's head, over which there was a cross.

"I was chosen by Mommy and Ralph," Parker said.

"Ralph!" Abby laughed. "Why don't you call him 'Daddy'?"

"Daddy," Parker said reluctantly.

"Why don't you call Mommy 'Joanne'?" Abby said.

"They got to *choose* me," Parker insisted.

"When you take a dump, do you save it in the bowl for Ralph to see before you flush it down?" Howard asked. "That's what I remember. The prominent throat specialist had to see mine and tell me it was good or it didn't go away. It *stayed* until the prominent throat specialist came home."

"Poor Howard," Caroline said. "That's what you remember?"

"Fondly," Howard said.

The guardian and his family were hammering away in the corrugated shed attached to their kitchen. Each night there was the sound of grinding and hammering. They made door knockers, June thought. But no one knew for certain. Those pretty door knockers in the shape of a lady's hand.

They began discussing, mostly for Parker's benefit, the rumors of a gringo ring that trafficked in the organs of Guatemalan children. This rumor had been around for years.

"There's a factory where the organs are processed," James said. "It's behind the video bar in Panajachel. It's just that everyone's too stoned to see it."

The gringo entrepreneurs didn't take the whole kid, they recounted loudly. Except in the beginning, of course. They took just a kidney or some tissue or an eye, which left the rest of the kid to get along as best he could, which usually wasn't very well.

"Parker," Howard said, "I hope Mommy and Ralph were sincere tonight as to their whereabouts. I hope they're not, in fact, kidnapping little Guatemalan children so they can have parts on hand for you, should any of your own parts fail. They could land in big trouble, Parker."

"I think he's asleep," James said.

"Wake up!" Howard roared. But Parker slept. Howard moodily raked his fire and then announced he was leaving to get some beer.

"I'll go with you," Abby said.

June would never have gone off alone with Howard. There was something cold and clandestine about him.

"What are you thinking, June?" James said after what seemed like a long while with Abby not yet back with Howard.

"I was thinking about that great, swaying float and how quiet everyone was when it passed."

"The *anda*," Caroline said. "The *anda de la merced*."

"That thing weighs three and a half tons," James said.

"It really was impressive, wasn't it?" June said.

"Well, duh," Caroline said. But she smiled at June as she said this.

"The drumrolls are still in my head," James said. "They provide the necessary cadences. The men probably couldn't bear it forward without those cadences being maintained."

"I can still hear the drumrolls too," June said gratefully.

"What's the word for the men who carry it?" James wondered. "I should keep a glossary."

"Cucuruchos," Caroline said. "One of them looked just like that cute dishwasher at the pizza place. I'm sure it was him."

"Look who we found!" Howard called from the gates.

It was the bottle boy from that morning, the one who'd eaten June's pancake.

"He was just outside," Abby said, "the beggar boy. Howard wanted him to share our picnic."

"He is not a beggar," Howard said. "His eyes lack the proper cringe. He is my brother, come to visit. That Bailey brat you met before was the false son and brother. A substitute substituted. Soul and body alike are often substituted." He was very drunk.

The boy was shivering. His shirt was torn and he wore a small silver cross around his neck. The shirt had not been torn that morning, June didn't think.

"Where's Parker's sweater?" Abby demanded. "I'm giving it to this one, that's what I'm going to do." She dug a red cable-knit sweater from Parker's bag and pulled it over the bottle boy's dark head, then pushed his arms through the sleeves. "I hope I don't get fleas now," she said.

Parker was sitting up and rubbing his eyes.

"Give him a sandwich," Caroline demanded.

Abby gave the bottle boy a sandwich thick with ham and cheese. He ate it slowly, watching them. Howard smoothed his fire with a stick. They drank beer.

"This is good," June said.

"It's the same kind we always drink," James said. "It's from Cuba."

They stood or sat drinking beer while the boy slowly ate the sandwich and watched them.

"I've been thinking about this for a while," Howard said. He threw his empty bottle down and pushed the sandals from his feet. "I have." He made fists of his hands, rolled his eyes upward and quickly walked the length of the fire pit.

"I don't believe it," Caroline said.

He turned and walked the fire again. "Cool moss," he screamed. "You think *cool moss*." He sank to the ground laughing, unharmed.

"You're loco," James said.

"Feel my feet, feel them," Howard said. "I ask you, are they hot?"

Caroline boldly touched the soles of his feet and pronounced them not warm at all. They were clammy, in fact.

"It doesn't have anything to do with belief," Howard said. "But if you have doubts, you burn. It's an evolutionary stimulant. I am now evolutionarily advanced."

"That is a fire that should so be put out right now," Abby said.

"I want to walk," Parker said. "I'm gonna walk." He stood and made small fists.

Abby yanked him toward her and slapped his bottom. "You are going to bed!" Abby said.

The fire winked radiantly at them all. Howard was laughing. He was deeply, coldly happy, and the revulsion June felt for him shocked her. She looked at Caroline uneasily.

"I do not believe this," Caroline said.

The Guatemalan boy had been collecting the empty bottles strewn about. He held them against his chest, against the bright red sweater. Then he put them down and, smiling furtively at Howard, stepped onto the fire. He screamed at once. Howard pulled him back, the boy screaming thinly. "You're all right, man, you're all right," he said, pouring beer over the boy's feet. "You were distracted and doubtful, man, and when you're D and D, you burn. *No tenga miedo. No es nada.*" He held the boy's feet and crooned *No es nada* to him in a mournful way, but he looked pleased.

Whimpering, the boy reached blindly for his bottles and clutched them once more to his chest.

"Get him out of here," Caroline said. "Give him the rest of the food. Give him the whole damn basket." She ran to the gates and opened them. "*Váyase! Váyase!*" she yelled at him.

As the boy stumbled out, he almost collided with the fortune birds being escorted home on their motorbike. The man of the remarkable vein steadied him with a snarl and then, regarding them all grimly, pushed the motorbike across the courtyard.

June ran up to him, digging coins from her pocket. "My fortune," she said, *"por favor."*

"In the morning," he said distinctly.

June looked closely at the tiny prophets clinging wearily to the bars of their cage, at their tiny egg-shaped breasts and dull feathers. Only a few rolled papers tied with rough string on the bottom of the cage.

"More in the morning," he said. "Better for you."

"No," June said. "I need it now. Morning no good. *No está bien,*" she said cautiously. "That one, Planeta, I want her to do it."

"Importa poco."

"What?" June said.

"It makes little difference."

"Planeta," she insisted. She pointed to the little one with the peeling bill and dark, opaque eyes that looked as though they'd been ringed in crayon.

"That is Justicio," he said. "Justicio," he sang softly, "Justicio . . ."

The bird dropped to the soiled floor of the cage and seized a tiny scroll as if it were a seed of much importance, a seed which could nourish it throughout the night. June pressed her fingers to the crookedly woven bars, almost expecting to receive a slight shock. The bird knocked the paper against her fingers. Once. Twice. She took it and the bird fluttered upwards to its perch, where it crouched like a clump of earth.

"Oh, June," Abby called. "What does it say?"

She turned toward her friends and walked slowly toward them, unrolling the paper. The writing was florid and crowded. There were many unfamiliar words. Caroline knew the language best, then Howard. What a mistake this had been! She would need time to study it and there was no time. Everyone was looking at her.

"Oh, it's just silly," she said, and threw it in the fire, where it burned sluggishly. No one attempted to retrieve it.

"God, isn't it late, where are my parents?" Abby said, yawning. "I want to go to bed."

June sat with them all a little while longer before going to her room. She lay on her bed discouraged, uncomfortably, listlessly awake. She heard a wailing from far away, but when she listened closely she could not hear it. She listened avidly now. Nothing. She could not recall the cadence of the drums. She had lied to James about that. But she could picture the *anda* being borne down the streets. That she would remember. It was fascinating to have seen the designs so meticulously created and then the *anda* passing, being borne on, swaying, and in its wake the designs smeared, crushed, a scattered wonder. And that part, after, had been fascinating too.

But she didn't really believe it was fascinating. It wasn't good to deceive yourself. She thought about Howard, hating him, and his cold grin. He was fleshy, did he not know that? Fleshier than most. He was not attractive. That was a lie, what Howard had done. It could hardly be anything else. She thought of the mannequins praying in their cell. A lie, too, but one that was funny. Things had to be funny.

. . .

In the morning, Caroline's dog was gone again. The rope had been knotted any number of times; it was always breaking. And when it broke, the dog would escape from the courtyard and, barking with joy, run through the streets. Caroline said that when it disappeared for good, it would be time to go. She had heard somewhere that angels tell you when it's time to leave a place by leaving just before you. June thought she had heard that too. Something like that.

A NOTE ON THE TYPE

This book was set in Adobe Garamond. Designed for the Adobe Corporation by Robert Slimbach, the fonts are based on types first cut by Claude Garamond (c. 1480–1561). Garamond was a pupil of Geoffroy Tory and is believed to have followed the Venetian models, although he introduced a number of important differences, and it is to him that we owe the letter we now know as "old style." He gave to his letters a certain elegance and feeling of movement that won their creator an immediate reputation and the patronage of Francis I of France.

Composed by Stratford Publishing Services,
Brattleboro, Vermont

Printed by R. R. Donnelley & Sons
Harrisonburg, Virginia

Designed by Pamela G. Parker